A BEGGAR'S TALES

A Beggar's Tales

A Novel

by

STEPHEN ERIC BRONNER

PELLA

PELLA PUBLISHING COMPANY

New York, NY 10001

1978

Library of Congress Catalog Card Number 78-060635

ISBN 0-918618-07-X Cloth
ISBN 0-918618-08-8 Paper

Printed in the United States of America
by
Athens Printing Company
461 Eighth Avenue
New York, NY 10001

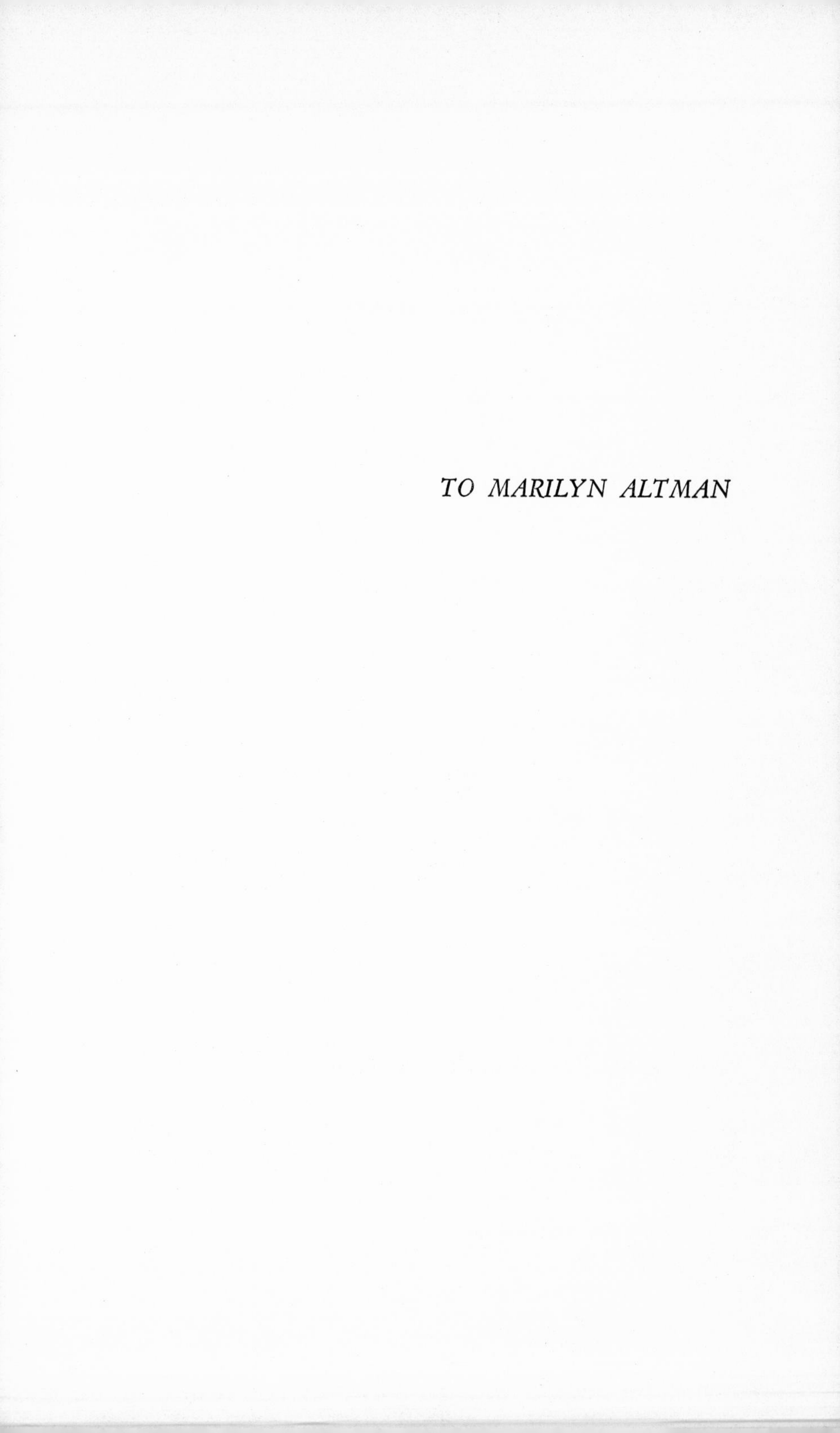

TO MARILYN ALTMAN

Prologue

Man is a god when he dreams, a beggar when he reflects.

—Hölderlin

NO! No need for introductions! Sit down! Come. Next to me. Closer! Ah! There we are! . . . You know, I have always liked cafés! But particularly in so overwhelming a city, with its massive buildings and lonely crowds, a place like this becomes absolutely essential. Only here, in such a place, can tales be told and myths be fostered; here, no one need feel constrained by his loneliness because everyone awaits a story.

Notice if you will, the café is almost full in spite of the hour . . . Few of the customers have anywhere to go. They talk, and they drink, and they listen. You see, for us there is no longer anything to do, and so everyone just waits—for stories.

Look over there! At that table! Two young ladies, and an overdressed young fool playing with a quarter; he's making it spin like a top, while attempting to flatten the coin as it twirls.

You think it's easy?

Try it some time and then let me know. Anyway, they say it's quite entertaining and perhaps that's why, almost every night, you can see a couple or two playing that little game. Look further and you'll see the card players. Of course, every café has its card players. But here they bet for penny stakes and the little fat one always loses. They play for hours on end and, when they finish, the little fat one quietly retreats to the bathroom where he swallows a pill and . . .

What do you mean, how do I know?

I know it for a fact! You see, I followed him once and... But why bother with that now? Better to look at that miserable group in the corner. They sit there every night and they always talk in the same languid manner. Their voices are low and their faces grim. But often—well, perhaps not that often—a glimmer of hope arises. It vanishes quickly of course, but for a single moment it shines with the stark purity of a pearl. Afterwards, naturally, each shows his embarrassment and looks around nervously until one of the group orders another decanter of wine.

Come to think of it, maybe I should order myself a drink. Yes, I find that my mouth is dry and my hands are wet and I have the distinct impression that this is not as it should be, eh?

Ah, ha! You laugh! So you do have a sense of humor! How you surprise me. You may rest assured that this will be a delightful evening!

—Waitress! *A double crème de menthe*—and you can put it on my bill.

—What?

—How dare you! Must I take my small request to the manager of this pedestrian establishment? Why, I'll...

—Now, that's better!

—Yes! I will control myself! May I ask when my behavior has not met with the highest standards of decorum?

—Ah, ha! There you are... and please be quick about it!

There's just no respect left! Why, a fellow has a few drinks and they begin to doubt his good will! Hmmph! the attitude of that waitress is enough to drive one... But I really shouldn't let myself be upset by such a trifle. Let me see, where was I?...

Oh, yes! Stories!.. I've heard so many. Each sounds so wonderful. In each the proper actions are always taken at the proper times and there is always a neat little theme. It's all so easy... But not my stories! No! No! In my stories, boredom can come too soon and action too late, despair too quickly and hope too... No! My stories are not packaged for consumption. They await the theme and only call forth the wonder which lies beneath an idea.

How strange they would seem to those sitting around other tables, these stories that one hears and then experiences as surely as if one had lived them oneself. They are stories which intangibly weave themselves into the pattern of an individual's existence. Stories of the night! Each rebuilds the skeleton of a life as it intensifies that moment which opens the world to one's eyes. Yes! In this transitory inactive world, a story at least can give rise to a moment of irrevocability. And that's all we have since . . .

You think not?

Well, I ask you, have you ever performed an irrevocable act?

So! You're not sure! But you know that you, too, will die and that this action should be irrevocable enough, eh?

Oh no, my friend! Irrevocability is a bit more difficult to achieve. There is nothing irrevocable about death! Give it a few years time and there won't be an inch of dirt that won't cover a grave. The fact that each of us has a coffin waiting is meaningless. Indeed, it offers no consolation whatsoever. For you see, what is irrevocable is not only what cannot be taken back but what must be preserved.

Listen to me! The irrevocable adheres to life, to each of us alone, and its outlines are barely visible—like last night's dream. Still, I have known men who have given up their lives, wasted their fortunes, and thrown away their souls for just a glimpse of the irrevocable. And alone, a glimpse is all one ever gets. One needs others and yet it's so difficult to find them. Just look around—the world is strewn with forgotten individuals: disparate, separate, a chaos of wasted dreams . . .

You don't understand?

Consider: did you or did you not have a great-great-great-great grandfather?

You suppose so?

Just as I suspected! You see now why I never lose an argument? Like the others, he is gone, forgotten. All that is left of what was his existence is a dream-like memory, nothing more than a supposition.

Well, it is precisely for suppositions like these that we have a café—a café in which through the telling of stories we make up for this deficiency caused by *supposing so.* Oh, they are rarely original and in fact, for the most part, they are nothing but lies. Yet in a way they serve the purpose, in this room where the interplay of shadows magnifies the thoughts in the air. This is the place we need: a room which turns into a cage, enclosing all of us (willing prisoners that we are!) in ash-gray lights reflecting off cheap marble table-tops, musty wine bottles, and the smells of cheap tobacco.

Yes, the atmosphere must . . .

No, my friend! Do not be put off! There is more to be said and much more to be seen. Hold on for just a moment, and I will make an introduction. But first, look about once more and notice the remnants.

Remnants of what?

But of course! Excuse me. You couldn't be expected to know that! After all, you weren't even here, were you? Well, in that case, please give me your undivided attention because I am going to tell you of an extraordinary event which occurred to me in this very place.

I was sitting right here, in this very spot, minding my own business—as I always do—when she came to me. She seemed to appear almost magically before me, and she has been with me ever since. What else could I call her but my Lady?

Now, have you ever been to Paris, *mon cher?*

No? More's the pity.

Well, had you gone, you would know that what was once Rodin's house is now a museum of his works. Outside lies what is grandiose, but inside, on the second floor, in an out-of-the-way corner, there sits a little statuette. Modelled after a poverty-stricken old woman of the last century, there—in that elegant old house—she rests, as obsequious as a trusted servant. One of the master's friends created her. Sculpted out of yellow marble, and perhaps a smidgen over a foot tall, it seemed that the artist saw fit to label his masterpiece *La Misère.*

But to me, she will always be the Lady! She is so old that one can feel the veins sticking out of her diseased hands. In the one she holds a staff and her nose, with a wart in the middle, enhances the gaze of her one good eye.

When she came, she leaned over to kiss me and slightly opened her toothless mouth which slowly twisted into a sneer. She whispered in my ear that she would return in a moment. She promised, my friend, and besides, she implied that I was something special to her and that, if I waited, she would tell me why.

With that, however, she seized her staff and smashed the skull of a rather portly fellow with a small goatee who was sitting at a table across from me. Then she kissed a woman full on the mouth and smeared the make-up of another. She cursed viciously and purposely instigated brawls.

She turned into an ogre—No, wait! A dragon! Yes, a dragon, lizard-like with green slimy scales, whose breath was like excrement. Swinging to and fro, her tail broke chairs and tables and her eyes sputtered with fire. She bit off an arm here, a leg there; she took chunks out of everyone in the room—that is, of course, except for me.

Now if you will be so kind as to move your chair around, you will be able to see the debris. As I am sure, however, that you yourself are a lover of the quieter pleasures, I have no doubt that you can imagine my horror. Oh, coward that I am, I despaired of flight! That is, until I was flung onto the hard pavement by the man in charge of this decrepit little tavern.

In the gutter my Lady was transformed into a vison of beauty; she tenderly crossed her smooth arms around me and touched my lips with a kiss. At that moment she became my lover—most wretched of lovers!—whose love I am still unable to escape; then she became the Lady I knew once again. Only she deceived me. She never told me why I was special; she has never uttered a word to me since, and still she is with me—as you see her now.

What do you say to that, eh?

So quiet?

But perhaps, dearest listener, you are suspicious of my choosing to disclose my most private thoughts and profound secrets?

No?

Well! You see, in order to gain a friend, or form an intimacy, curiosity must be awakened. Before all else, one must give the other a taste—just a taste, mind you!—of one's soul; it must be a taste which will implant on the listener's palette a precious moment or two from the life of another.

You see, each of us has a craving for *the new*, a desire to extend one's vision. And yet, for the most part, it all remains dormant. The hope for the new continues to smoulder, but we temper it with the certainty of the present.

And the reason? We have lost the ability to hope and so we can no longer even conceive of a future which is different from the present. Yes, we have been taught to accept the contours of the existent. And so, manacled to what we have been taught we are, we resign ourselves to what we will be by displacing our actions into dreams and our dreams into stories.

It makes sense too! My Lady knows that in creating a world, as in creating a theme, there is always the threat of turmoil. And then, too, what we have seems so secure and the stories which we always hear are so very safe.

Thank God for stories! At least they give us a sense of the moment!

What moment?

Any moment! It doesn't have to be unique! It needn't even be the least bit interesting for its own sake! It need only snatch one from the tedium of existence.

But to do this, the moment must beckon—and yet be fixed; it must be frozen with each detail clearly in place. Yes! It must be frozen like a scene painted by Vermeer—a scene of clarity, purity and translucent purpose. But then, Vermeer is of an age that is long past and, after all—as my Lady had always believed!—why should what was important for him remain equally important for us, eh?

But that's neither here nor there. Innumerable times questions arise for which we have no answers at hand. Then we must be prudent; we must learn how to wait, sit back and cultivate our patience as we tend to more salient matters.

—How marvelous! The drink looks simply wonderful, and with crackers besides! You really are delightful . . .

Ahem! I beg your pardon, dearest friend. Would you believe that I once knew a girl who looked very much like this waitress? She had herself committed because she needed someone to love her. A very nice girl she was too. She was fairly attractive and reasonably intelligent, of unpretentious character and moderate means. She searched for five years and found no one.

But I know that you have heard it all before. So you must realize that it is only in the telling—in the reflection of my face upon your eyes—that this moment, this tale which binds us, may be preserved.

Yes, lacking all other means, this is how a man such as myself propagates the irrevocable. For, in a moment, we have come to be united and perhaps a treasure lies hidden in our communion. Who can say? For now, we know only the joy of anticipation—but that should suffice.

All right, it's true! In a certain sense, the irrevocable does feed off some unknown soul's struggle with misery. But that is only part of it. There's more as well . . . If I . . . Were there only something which I could do! You see, there's a hope, a dream which I have never quite been able to formulate . . . At times, I even thought there was a chance to . . .

Not so fast! I still have been able to achieve a certain stature! Look at me, my friend! For me, even the soft features of the fair sex have lost their allure; as for liquor, why, you can see for yourself that it's just a passing fancy, and money . . . Well, my Lady taught me long ago that one finds comfort where one imagines it to be.

You see, through the stance that I take, I have come to grips with this world of horrors, and as for the others . . . Oh, I have heard them! Those who always invoke the struggle of the masses in the fight with a god who is kept in the heavens. To each other they speak of oppression and corruption . . . Actors, poets, priests and vagabonds, who speak with nothing but the inner certainty of knowledge. Grimy and righteous, offer them a job on a silver platter and they'll turn it down. No doubt they themselves don't know why this mass of theirs turns its back on them. But turn its back on them it does and quietly, standing on the graves of its fathers, chooses to wait.

And why not? Like myself, these orators have nothing to be ashamed of. In the most somber and urgent tones they speak of the great problems which plague 'our' times—as if there is some kind of 'brotherhood' which presumably makes them 'ours.' And they follow it all with a marvelous revue!

Ah! It makes me think of those wonderful ancients who made sure that at festivals a comedy would be presented only after the tragedy so that the populace would sleep soundly at night. And I remember how the new age progressed as *sensitivity* demanded that the oppressed turn their grandest opportunity into a soap opera of inwardness. And what a soap opera it was: a little bit of acting, a little bit of politics, a little bit of singing, a little bit of blood. Foolishness! Idiocy! Naiveté! Raucous mobs on the street! Riots! Chaos! It's all pure nonsense, far beneath the dignity of a man such as myself.

One would think that people would have come to their senses. But now even what little there was is gone. There is only a suffocating languor which pervades our world. So I turn to my Lady and I find new hope! I find that boredom is as valid a motive for discontent as any other if—as with ourselves, my friend!—boredom is imbued with the will to create. Alone, apart from the mob, one can . . .

I have learned my lesson well! First the proper level of inwardness must be achieved. The soul of a man is what counts! Indeed, we must be exact!

Yes, my love, I was just about to ask how anyone else is to create anything if he is unable to explain why I use a cigarette holder, let alone manipulate it in that inimitable way of mine.

— Waitress, do you like it? Yes, you exquisite creature! It's made out of the purest ivory and was given to me by a slave trader who, in his youth, aspired to poetry. Magnificent, is it not? Carved from the tusk of a white elephant by an eighty year old savage! Clearly the object is priceless! But, as I have always felt a deep attachment for you, I might just be willing to let it go for . . .

—No?

—Well, I can only say that it's your loss. Still, should you reconsider...

The impertinence of that waitress! These interruptions are terribly disconcerting, I know. But, now then, what is there left for me besides these tales told in the night?

A family you say?

Why, those children I have known were, from their infancy, the nastiest of brats. I tell you that most of them even crawled with the sly look of thieves. And marriage?.. Isn't it amazing how good they look the first time you see them? How their faces take on that certain glow from the match waiting for a cigarette? How they seem to have that air of depth and kindness about them, and how they make you believe that the smile is reserved for you?.. Ah, yes!

But it's all so transitory, barely even a memory capable of turning into an illusion. Anyway! What use have I of illusions, or memory for that matter? A memory is what we mold, what we create, only to take as gospel—and all to suit our whims. For who wants an unpleasant memory, eh? It only bequeaths an anguish without form—a horror which can never be realized in its fullness.

No! Taking such a situation seriously leaves one only the choice between trusting oneself and becoming a mental flagellant—and I can do neither. What's more I am a man of no age, of no imagination; I am a man who chooses to resist both the fact and that vague potential for transcendence within it. I, whose passion transcends time and the world, am infused only with a story and the moment. And that moment glistens!

You see, it isn't true what they all say! I will never be a poet of retreat! In truth, my tales preserve the prospect of utopia—a specter which hovers on the other side of all the mangled dreams covered with slime... But I was never one to clear swamps, so look into my words, into the filth, and there the gems will be found; they will glow when the sights are ugliest, they will beckon when the stench is strongest. Stay with me and perhaps you might even wish to stick your own hands into the muck to retrieve a...

So, you ask if these tales are true?

How can I say, when I'm not even sure if these tales are my own?

You see, from my chair I watch for the silhouettes beyond the flesh of those who cross my path, those into whom I might extend my spirit.

Long ago the streets turned cold. But there is always the crowd of the café. In the face of inaction I abandon myself to them, suck in their experiences, their actions and their dreams, until finally they become mine as what is my own becomes unwittingly theirs.

Ask my Lady! Ask her and perhaps she will tell you that this is how one expands beyond the narrow boundaries of the body. For in my tales there are no bodies. There are only silhouettes; silhouettes which turn on me, torment me and laugh—laugh without mercy. Still, they grant me a certain experience. You see, I find that through this entourage of silhouettes—without even attempting to act—I can momentarily touch the fabric of history.

Often it's horrible! Even on the day when I rejoiced to hear that some malicious little monster died in what remained of a corporal's cloak inside a blown-out bunker—everyone in the café only laughed. And in their laughter my joy turned into an illusion of bliss. Each atrocity, every look in the maniac's eyes was imperceptibly banished and—God help me!—for an instant I thought that, in this very place, a new more insidious horror would be resurrected. For I know that sitting can become a habit and that, at times, even passive dreaming can become a curse.

Of course, I knew even then that the semblances would fade, that the silhouettes would vanish, and that reality would finally enter this café where a precarious laughter breathes. I looked around at the faces and I knew, too, that by that time it would be too late.

Well, there was nothing to be done. I went home and even long afterwards I found myself thinking occasionally of that moment. But it's so very long ago. You see, this moment too was forgotten—even by the silhouettes—and now only a vague discomfort bears witness to the actual remembrance.

Time plays its pranks, but I sometimes think that it also demands a reckoning. Perhaps there remain some unhealed scars left from earlier moments—moments of beauty which were never actualized, moments of terror which were never exorcised, moments which strain against the surface of existence. And if a day should ever come when they might break through, a day when dreams and stories will no longer be enough, well then . . .

Ah! How I know! When the beginnings of a vision tempt one and the dream becomes both a solace and a threat . . . Alone, one can immerse oneself in a dream and this vision may serve to protect one even from the blandness of death . . . And yet I know that it is only when the dream of tomorrow is set free through action that *the new* truly begins to sparkle and that the horizon opens up for the grandest experience. Then! . . But now . . . The lethargy which stalks in our midst is a wily enemy and the faith in affluence is a strong and resilient opponent. A battle is no small thing with these guardians of the gate—and there is always the thought that the guardians might triumph.

And what then, you ask?

Then? . . Then these guardians will show no mercy! Benevolence will turn into anger, tolerance into horror. Chains will abound, ovens will glow, and blood will stream through the streets while a new monster claps with joy as he peeks out over his balcony.

So you see, I understand it all. The stakes are high and, then too, for a man such as myself these types of odds are . . .

— What?

— Not now! Isn't there the least bit of decency left in this decaying world? Don't you think that you can show me the check a bit later on?

Good, she's gone—at least for a while. So, if you have some time, perhaps I might suggest listening to some of the tales which were told to me on a night in the not very distant past. After all, we have barely met and I can already see that you have become a connoisseur of the moment.

Part One

I

SO you are still here! How wonderful! You see, I know that it's a difficult thing to arouse one's interest in anything—particularly when one is alone. And how much more difficult it must be to act alone? One must have quite a dream before action can be undertaken. To choose alone! To make the unique choice which precedes even the thought of acting with others! To stand alone with a choice that can never be completely justified! And yet it must be justified if one is not to go mad!

Now what better way of justifying anything than through a story, a simple story which begins in the most ordinary way. Take a night not so very long ago. That dark haired little boy—over there in the doorway!—came in to sell his papers. Every evening he follows the same routine with the late edition. He'll peek inside the entrance to see if the manager is around. Then he'll breathe a loud sigh of relief and, with a gleam in his eye, come over to offer me the first copy.

Watch, here he comes!

— No, I do not! Even were I to bother with newspapers I certainly wouldn't read that rag which you're selling!

— What?

— Why don't you go back to school and learn to read before

you incite others to fill their minds with such trash?!

—School's out, you say?

— I'll stand for none of your cheek, young man! Why, I have a good mind to speak to the manager about you . . .

— How dare you!

— In my time a child your age didn't even know what that meant! Get away from me or I'll . . .

Dirty little rodent! Imagine making a gesture like that in public!

— Go ahead! Laugh, you senile old coot!

The same old wretch is always laughing—and he laughed on that night too! But now I can ignore his laughter. Each of us has a story to tell, yet once it's told . . .

On that night, for some reason, I could not endure his laughter—and so I confronted him. Gaily, he invited me to join him and proceeded to explain that he would never presume to laugh at me.

Now, I have always been a trusting soul and—since a drink was placed before me—I decided to hold my peace. He began to talk about the uprisings which had recently swept the world and how he hated the infirmities brought on by old age. Then he looked over at the child selling his papers and told me that he too had once sold newspapers in the street. From what he said, selling newspapers was apparently a weary business and it became clear that, as a child, the fellow took the job against the advice of his grandfather.

His grandfather! . . What a man this relative of his must have been! Why, I can tell you in all truth that I have rarely learned more from a person I have never known!

Physically, his grandfather must have been enormously powerful for it was rumored that the old man had once lifted a fair-sized cow. And his face! I see it before me! It makes me think of the face of a horse: long, flat, rectangular, and besides, it seems that the old man had a habit of breathing through his nose . . .

Whenever my companion saw him the old man had the shadowy stubble of a beard—and how he could talk! My acquaintance told me that his grandfather's intonation would rise and fall like a melody, reach the peak of a crescendo and then become very soft.

From what I inferred, the old man mixed his phrases in a strange way; in seconds he could move from the slang of the gutter to poetry. Brutally articulate, his sentences would nonetheless somehow remain open; they always seemed to linger, waiting for the next context in which they would become appropriate.

The old man possessed little formal schooling. Still, he managed to read a bit here and there although the gaps in his knowledge were enormous. The old man knew it too, and he was always a bit defensive. Often, in fact, he would try to parade his ignorance as a testament to the experiences he had undergone in the world. But he was also deeply ashamed of such behavior and wouldn't hesitate to ridicule those who acted in the same manner. Scattered though his knowledge was, however, he was still somehow able to mold it into a world-view—a world-view which served as a guide to action.

Yes, action was always uppermost in his mind, and there was nothing which he could accept passively. Sailor, porter, trackman: he had travelled all over the globe. He had been to Asia and had wept over the women whom he had seen with their feet crushed into little balls; he had screamed with horror in that small restaurant when Jaurès was assassinated; and he felt himself nearly burst inside when he met Trotsky while working at a department store in New York.

Only later did he go to see the revolution which shook a half-barbaric country with the force of a typhoon. But everywhere he went he allied himself with those who wanted to own the means by which the world's wealth was produced. Always he walked the thin line between apocalypse and reform: equality meant Morgan's head on a platter, but he was no man to spit on whatever could alleviate misery—even if only for a moment. He wasn't a pacifist either, he knew that blood needed to be shed, and yet he realized that the only justification for that was the creation of a bond among those through whom the free and *the new* might be realized.

The colors black and red dominated his travels, his hopes and his life. Everywhere he found their traces and he revelled in the spark which appeared in Russia and, for a moment or two, flickered in Europe only to spring up again in China when the world had thought it dead in Spain. Yes, he revelled in the change, half-feared it, waited for it in the country of his birth—and saw it vanish.

But the child never knew any of this first-hand. All that he saw before him was an incurably sick old man. Yet the child would always go to his grandfather's room with the large candelabra, the thick brocade curtains and the fake Persian carpet to listen to the old man's stories. In that room, tucked in a canopied bed, the old man lay with yellowish rings around his eyes. Often, the child heard nothing other than disconnected ramblings, but when these ramblings finally took shape . . . The old fellow sitting across from me on that night said that he would never forget the one about people gathered around a table.

This one's just up your alley, my Love! For it seems that someone suggested that each tell the others what he would ask were he to be granted one wish.

The first, a wealthy manufacturer of ladies' underwear, responded: "a long and healthy life."

The second, a singularly untalented artist, answered: "fame."

The third, a pock-marked little clerk, said: "the wife of my boss."

The fourth, however, a poor man who had been unemployed for most of his life and who suffered from asthma and astigmatism, looked away from them and began to smile: "What I would wish for would be a beautiful house in which the most beautiful paintings would come to life. There would be a garden filled with a thousand different flowers and I would have a wife with lovely black hair whom I would love very much. There would be work, but I would be owned by no one, and there would be no need for charity. There would always be clumps of stars in the sky and something exciting to do so that, though I might remain mortal, the fear of death would be conquered. Perhaps we might even speak in song or poetry. All the battered dreams of the past would exist for you and me together and there would be . . ."

The old man said that this fellow went on for close to an hour, that he could have gone on for even longer, but that finally the others stopped him; they had grown weary of the game.

"You see," the old man said, "fellows like him often tend to think about questions like these more than others. For people like him, it can never be a game."

Oh, my Lady, how the child must have loved the way the old fellow talked. Throughout the story the child must have felt the old man sparkle. But a certain desperation was also apparent. The old man wished to put so much into his words—and yet, he knew that grandeur could not simply be spoken.

For him, however, there was little else to do except speak. It seemed to the child that the old man had been ill for years. Since he could remember, the old man's eyes had been glazed and his cheeks abnormally flushed. But gradually the old man came to eat less and as he began to lose weight his skin began to sag. He grew tired ever more easily and yet on the day that they put him to bed . . . Well, they nearly had to chain him down. There, lying on his back, he grew weaker still as each moment drew him further into the shadow of that terrible sickness.

And yet, that was not the worst of it! There was more. Always there was the thought: that *they* should be witness to this! That those relatives of his should see him so! Spread-eagled like a wretched beggar in his utter helplessness.

For the first time, the family was able to see him fight; only this time against a force which he had no hope of conquering. The old man was unable to tolerate such a thought—and for this, he hated them.

I would imagine that one would have had to be deaf not to detect this hatred in the murmurings which broke through his pain. And his illness was painful—no doubt about that! Whenever he tried to shift his body he would grimace and, once in a while, let out the heavy groan which he had so often held back. Sometimes in the morning there would be flecks of blood on his pillow. But there were also the minor aches, the bedsores, the discomfort, the boredom—and, then too, the thoughts of that medicine which he had to take every hour on the hour.

That dull brown vial! How well my companion recalled it, sitting there on the shelf next to the French windows. The contents looked like phlegm, viscous and green, thick with the prescient smell of nausea. Each time it was given to him the veins in the old man's face grew ready to burst and he would have a fit of coughing and then pitiably try to vomit. Often the child would catch him lying gazing at the bottle. There, in that little flask, stood what was left of his future and the weary invalid would stare at it with the same careful disgust with which he looked at his son, the child's father.

"What a boy my father must have been," my acquaintance exclaimed. It seemed that the son had studied hard to become a broker and had worked in the same firm for years. There was little resemblance between the son and the old man. The son's wife had died while the child was still in its infancy—and so the son was free to dominate this house where a child was waiting to mature and an old man was waiting to die.

Secure in his little house, the son had slowly accumulated a bit of money which he cautiously proceeded to invest. His money grew, but it never grew quite enough for him to actually enter that world of wealth of which he had always dreamed.

Yet, the son had something while the old man had nothing. As a result, the son could look at his father and see before him a wasted life which gave meaning to his own. The old man's burden had to be borne—and was borne graciously by the son to all appearances. But, strange though it was, it seemed that the old man's illness somehow gave way to the son's sense of sacrifice: the type of sacrifice which allowed the son to make clear his disapproval of the old man without appearing callous.

The child watched while the son sat with the assorted aunts, uncles, and nephews, to wait the end of this man whom they barely new and hardly liked. The aunts, uncles and nephews . . . Well, they hadn't laid eyes on the old man in decades, but they came nonetheless as if drawn by the scent of death.

The old man had given up on all of them. Within minutes of their arrival, he would claim an intense weariness and ask to sleep. The old man had even given up on his son. As a youth, the old man had tried to hold his son close. But the old man was always moving and, by the time his son had entered the university, there was no longer even the hope of a bond between them. The son could not dissociate himself quickly enough from the ways of his errant father. When the son graduated, he and his fiancée gave a little party; the old man was not invited even though he certainly would not have gone.

The old man was perceived as a man without a home, without a homeland, without roots or friends of the proper sort. His travels, his battles, his politics, his co-workers and his dreams—all that which fascinated the child—were seen as nothing but a fool's dreams, an idiot's idealism. The old man despised them and they pitied him for it. Yes, they pitied him—at least in the beginning. But even pity can be crushed under the burden of care.

Imagine! To be dependent on them! To owe each day to a group of self-righteous automatons who would pay every bill, and always with the same dour look of dismay. The more the old man's strength was sapped from him, the costlier he—this half-alive commodity—became.

And, of course, he knew it! He felt it in the way that they glared at him, spoke kindly to him, fed him, and screwed up their noses when they changed his sheets. Thus, for the child, life in the little house with the brocade curtains imperceptibly began to turn more and more into an existence lived between hostile camps with a common objective.

The old man wanted to die and the relatives wanted him to die as well. But they sustained him with their medicine, which was demanded by their law, which somehow always became caught up with their deity. Ordered to dispense the medicine to him, they proceeded to do so—hour after hour, waiting for the clock to drink the time.

The old man had told the child that he wished to die. Alone, without a friend, the child had become the old man's only confidant and the old man admitted to him that it was not death, but only the pain which he feared. Half with loathing, half with awe, the old man awaited the pain and then succumbed to its fury. He was wracked with pain and death appeared before him in a savior's guise; for all else lay behind him and there was only more pain ahead... That was it! That alone. The pain. But no! Wait! That was not it! There was one thing more. The thought of God!

Now, now, my Lady! Not so quick with your glee! His concern was not quite as trite as one might be led to expect. The thoughts of the holy which he pursued in his idleness always led back to the child.

One day, you see, it seems that the child was left with the old man and told to make sure that he be given his medicine on the hour. Thinking he was asleep, the child entered the old man's room on tiptoe. But the old man's eyes were open and, looking at the young boy as if he were glaring into time's mirror, he motioned the child to come close. Trying to lift his head, the old man spoke with the shadow of a grin.

"They tell you about God, don't they?" And, without waiting for the child to respond, he continued. "And that's why they won't let me die. Well, I've had a bit of time to think about Him, and do you know what I've decided? I've decided that it would be quite a joke if there were something out there. Imagine, some character actually lounging around up there pulling his invisible puppet strings... What a bastard! What a vain bastard He'd be!"

And then he looked at the child imploringly. "You've got to know that He'd be a bastard! Worse than any dictator!

"Don't say a word! I know! You've been told that He gave us freedom. But that's nonsense. His freedom is nothing but an illusion. Let the scholars debate, but as far as I can see, no matter how you cut it, if He's up there, we exist for Him. At least with a real dictator you know where you stand, but with Him... Don't you see that the freedom which He gives is never the freedom to reach His heights?

"If He's up there, then He's a tyrant, that's for sure! You remember that Tower of Babel? Look at what He did to it? What He did to those people, because they said, let me see... Yes! 'Go to, let us build a city and a tower, whose top may reach unto heaven.' Because they dreamed of that, because they dreamed of a better world—and acted upon the dream!

"No! If He's up there, *that* one must never attempt to do! To dream, to act, to create! To 'reach unto heaven!' And my companion remembered how he had maintained that there was creation before the Tower, though he told me that his grandfather only shrugged at his words.

"You're right," the old man said. "There was creation before. I know my Bible! Altars had already existed, sacrifices had already been made. But something made in order to honor man himself, something in which people could see themselves, and their lives, and their hopes... No, no! That had never been attempted before and how could this have failed to offend the Lord? That workers should work for themselves, that a creation should exist for its creators! The Lord has made this dream taboo and, let me tell you child, this taboo has been carried over into the world of men!"

With those words, he looked at the door. "Out there... They pray for me, eh?"

What else could the child have done, my friend, but nod his head in the affirmative?

"I'll bet!" he went on. "Those vultures, they hate me and, if they had the nerve to take a chance, they'd bury me tomorrow. But they're cowards and they'll get nothing from me! No inheritance. Nothing!.. Perhaps it's too bad that..." But he was already out of breath. He coughed thickly and, when he brought himself under control, delirium clouded his eyes.

"Ah, to hell with them! Ignore them! When I die," and the old man would not let himself be interrupted, "when I die, don't contradict them. Let them do what they want, say what they want. Let them eulogize me to the Lord and then breathe their sighs of relief. But you, you remember! Remember what I say to you now! If there is a God, if I meet Him in a day or two, remember that I only hope for one thing—I hope that I have strength enough, and get near enough to Him, to piss on his foot."

I swear to you that my companion—now pitiably old himself—burst out laughing until tears streamed down his face.

It seems that he had laughed like that in front of his grandfather too and that the old man had laughed with him. But then his grandfather began to cough once again. Terror seized the child, but the old man overcame his spasm. Then, in an affectionate voice, he said:

"You and I, my boy, we understand each other. You've got some common sense and you even know how to laugh. But them . . . Blach!"

Even you, my Darling, could not have restrained yourself!

The youth laughed again, for there was no other word which the old man could have substituted. That gutteral sound of disgust conveyed a specific form and content to what the child saw as the enemy.

The child reflected: either they whined or they complained or, when they dared, snickered with their teeth clenched. Carefully, and with due humility, they always contrived to do what they were told—and no more than that—with the least amount of exertion. To each other, the cries of their indignation—regarding everything in general and nothing in particular—would carry through the halls of that splendid little house. But in public . . . Well, then they would lower their voices and creep along with a silent tread. They would obediently follow their affluent road to oblivion; with their dignity sold they would follow the same road on which untold generations had been led from time immemorial.

And the child wished to rebel. He promised himself that he would not be like them: those who had let their hands be tied and who refused to think about the knots tearing into their flesh. And the child experienced a hope which was only inflated when he heard the old man shout:

"To hell with their prayers! I see the fire in your eyes and I know that you won't pray. But be careful, that I tell you, because they'll know that you're not praying. Be silent, because they'll never forgive . . . no, they'll never forgive you if you tell them that it's all for nothing should the invisible puppeteer actually exist.

"Life only counts when you look to men. When you look to them in their evil and misery and stupidity and occasional moments of decency and grandeur! You can only look to them, otherwise . . .

"Listen to me. I worked when I had to, was good to the people I liked and fought against those who would deny me and those like me. Occasionally I woke up believing that I would sleep with anything that had four legs or under, and often, when I was travelling, I would shiver from the cold and sweat from the heat. Other times I'd be dead tired and wouldn't be able to sleep at all. But even then I would sometimes feel my imagination break free! Thoughts, wonderful, striking thoughts would slip in and out of my mind. Damn! If only I could recapture those thoughts from the mist and hand them over to you! Yes, those beautiful thoughts of what might be, with which I grappled when sleep was just beginning during those times when I found myself stranded between darkness and light.

"All that, it's mine! It belongs to me! But don't you see that it's only really mine if there is no God and if only men exist?

"O.K. I'm not much. I have nothing to leave you except a memory. But if men—and what they built—created what I became, then at least I can throw my curse on those responsible. The rich . . . Ha! They never knew me from Adam—but I knew them, and others like me know them too! The monuments which were chiseled for them, the ideas which were conceived for them, the conditions that they formed—I tasted all of that, if only from afar. If all this belongs to some men, then others can claim it for themselves.

"But if this doesn't belong to men, if it *is* God who is responsible, then it belongs to Him alone. Then freedom is worthless and the struggle is worthless too. Because finally the real goal of the struggle is that everything created must belong to the creators—everything, in its entirety. Don't you see? If God exists then even my own life doesn't belong to me. If I find a God where I'm going then I'll know that those ejaculations weren't actually mine at all, but rather an extension of His own: I'll know that the dreams I dreamed and the actions I performed were nothing more than a game, a set-up, for the whims of a despot who played me like a fiddle."

The sick old man kept talking, but my acquaintance couldn't remember what he said. Most of it was probably incoherent anyway. And so the child stopped listening and concentrated on the clock.

"High time for the old man's medicine," the child thought. Then he walked over to the shelf and took the bottle. Holding it in one hand, and a shiny spoon in the other, the child felt a weakness in his arms. He was about to remove the cap from the bottle, but then—just at that moment—the old man began to speak once more.

"All my comrades are gone. I'm alone, just like you. Perhaps you'll find new ones, they'll have hopes for you . . . But in order to realize those hopes you'll have to understand what action means. Maybe . . . maybe I can show you . . . show you by giving myself over to you."

Ah, my friend! Need I tell you how the old man's words must have affected the child? How he must have stood there spellbound as he realized that it had to be then if it was to be at all? The moment in which the child could save him was almost past. The child tilted the bottle and the spoon trembled in his hand. But he didn't tilt the bottle far enough; the liquid remained in the flask and the moment passed. Surely the old man must have seen the child's face drop and, with a smile, said:

"After I'm gone you'll be the one to reconstruct my life and you'll need a touch of imagination to tie the loose strands together . . . A touch of imagination, that's all that can help you when you're alone, when you have no comrades. Search them out. If you find them, then perhaps you'll be able to do what really needs to be done. This is only a first step. But at least now you know that, even alone, there is an act, a favor which . . ."

A favor! That was what the old man called it and my companion's face flushed as he recalled the moment. Can you imagine? Murder, the most heinous of crimes, a favor—and yet, it was a favor.

By the time the child's father returned, the old man was

dead. The child had remained in his grandfather's room humming a tune which he had heard on the radio that morning. He had watched the old man's spasms grow more frequent, watched him shudder and watched his eyes close. There were few words exchanged with the others when they arrived. Everyone appeared sober and no one was particularly shocked. Now and then, someone cried softly into a handkerchief, but there was no sobbing and no words were caught in anyone's throat. The funeral was held shortly thereafter and it passed without incident. As they lowered the casket into the ground, the child heard his father tell him to be brave. The child thought of the old man, of future comrades, and of the dream and the act which hovered on an uncertain horizon.

This was how my companion finished his tale. Then, this aging man looked at me quizzically, expectantly, waiting for me to . . . But I glanced over at my Lady and remained silent. It was only after a moment or two that my companion wearily shook his head and moved to another table.

II

There you have it! A story has been told! In an instant, God and innocence have been expelled from the world! All that remains is a knowledge of the possibility for action and the need for choice.

But wait! It often happens that I speak too soon! For there are some who will not even choose their comrades. In fact, I know that there are those who seek to preserve their innocence by extending their sympathy to everyone. What about them, my friend? It's a question which my previous story doesn't answer.

Yet, now you can see how stories begin to form a network, how one story ends where another begins, until finally a surrogate existence is created. But the final product takes some time to evolve and one must not be too impatient! The process advances slowly, step by step . . . And so now we must return to the question of what happens to those who refuse to discriminate in choosing the objects of their sympathy.

Those who believe in an equality of sympathy are an extraordinary lot and we might do well to consider a former friend of mine. In certain respects he was much like the old man; he too had seen a good deal and had held many jobs. When he was young he owned an ice cream truck and I remember him happily jingling the bells which would announce his arrival to the anxiously awaiting children. But, as fate would have it, he chose to drive without insurance.

Ah! He made little enough as it was. So, when the truck was demolished in an unfortunate accident, he was forced to take a job in construction. While he was employed there, however, no one awaited him with expectant glee and, little by little, he felt the city begin to smother him. He moved on and, by the time he was done, he had crossed the width of the country. For a time he worked as a garbage collector, then as a dishwasher, and once he was even charged with feeding the elephants in a travelling circus; he picked fruit in a sun which made the leaves brittle, packaged meat in an ice-cold factory, and ultimately even served as a prison guard.

When one is fit for nothing there is no reason why one shouldn't try his hand at everything, eh? Thus the little fellow gained experience, the experience which he believed enabled him to understand *the nature* of human existence. Because of what he had seen this sensitive individual never indulged himself in visions of *the new*. For his experience had taught him that suffering alone defined existence—an anguished suffering which each undergoes in the privacy of his heart. Sometimes I think that he should have become a priest, for the heart alone mattered to him and that's why this little fellow never bothered to ask how it came to be that one man was richer than another in both body and mind. All that concerned him was *the experience of suffering* and he sought to alleviate this as well as he could—as one man to another.

And no favorites would be played! Suffering was suffering! No external trappings could change that! For suffering was *internal* and, in the face of this eternal suffering, all outward differences vanished. For him there were no classes, no races, no oppressors, no oppressed; there were only men and women—individuals—each a part of the universe of suffering.

So, you find it odd that a fellow such as he should have chosen to become a prison guard?

Well, with what could have been the light touch of my Lady's fingers, one day a newspaper appeared in his hands. You see, he always found newspapers to be a pleasant distraction. But, at the time, this was particularly the case since the town in which he found himself was barren and cold, located somewhere in the midst of a vast prairie. He occupied a room in a shabby hotel, where he often stood by the window. All that he could see was land: land with a highway slicing through its middle, land without a hill or a valley, smooth land, continuous and expanding. In just this way, his country became visible to him. Abandoned, he saw himself as a speck of dust in a desert. Finally, he was unable to stand the sight any longer and, as he shifted his head, the classified ad flashed before his eyes. On the next day, he appeared at the warden's office.

Although others may have thought this warden severe, the little fellow found him honest and sensitive. The warden spoke softly and made clear his concern for his prisoners. He spoke of how hard it must be for them and how their plight must be recognized by the staff in its dealings with its "clientele." The little fellow was greatly impressed. He knew that the warden and he would become friends. As for the warden, he liked the stranger's manner, his unsophisticated charm and that intense concern for others which lacked any form of condescension.

A man without bitterness or arrogance, so the warden must have thought. A man who, most probably, in his simple way and after his own fashion, would do what he could to make the lives of those around him a bit more pleasant. The warden asked him to wait outside, ran a check, and then ushered him back inside. The little fellow was hired on the spot.

In the beginning, of course, the little fellow felt strange. Unseen eyes spied on him from everywhere and the weight of the gun in the leather holster felt uncomfortable against his leg. Then too, there were the iron bars, the bareness of the floors and walls, the drabness of the gray uniforms, and the sullenness of the men in his charge; everything served to unsettle this most decent individual.

Still, he never tried to disguise his uneasiness and the prisoners took notice of the timid politeness with which he spoke to them. They noticed everything; the kindness, the growing sympathy and the peculiar reverence before suffering which—they thought—marked him as one of them. Cautiously, they inched closer to him. They were attracted by his naive candor when he asked their advice on women and soon they found themselves going to him when they had disagreements. He was an honest man and it was easy for him to be fair.

The warden couldn't have been happier with his new employee. They had lunch twice a week and the little fellow came to know of the warden's dear mother, of his hard-working uncle, of some family skeletons, and of his daughter, of her success, of her anguish and her broken love affair. Only rarely did the warden speak about the prison and this impressed the little fellow even more. The better he came to know this warden, the more amazed he was at this man who bore such awesome responsibility without a murmur of complaint.

So, one month turned into the next. Time passed uneventfully—that is until, late one night, a prison break occurred. My acquaintance was not to be found amidst the confusion: he had withdrawn into the background.

No! Do not misunderstand! It wasn't a question of cowardice. Not at all! He purposely moved into the shadows where he sorrowfully stood pitying guards and prisoners alike. But his eyes were fixed on the ground. There, a round drop of thin red fluid, the end of a liquid thread, was coagulating. Following its course backward, it led to a puddle of blood. A guard had staggered up to that point; now he was a corpse which would suffer no more.

The little fellow had known the body when it had been alive. In fact, he had just been talking to it—about the menu, I think he said—when the insurrection broke out. The corpse lay sprawled, limp, and pallid, with one eye closed. Soon it would begin to stink, begin to give off that paste-like odor of decomposition.

The little guard had seen two prisoners shot; but that had occurred far away on the other side of the courtyard. This corpse, however, lay right before his eyes. At first it absorbed him, but then he began to hate it. For just a moment, a truly ferocious hatred overcame him; death took shape and emerged as an affront, an unwarranted insult to his very being.

Ah, my Lady! On the day after, it was as if his hatred had been spent on that inert lump of flesh. He showed no malice to the prisoners, the guards or the warden. In fact, the prisoners were nothing less than astounded that this guard did not reproach them for their actions. In contrast to his colleagues, neither a grumble nor a curse was to be heard from the little guard—not a word about the dead, about the added inspections, the reports that had to be filled out, the extra training sessions, or anything else.

The little fellow didn't like the way in which the other guards took out their anger on the prisoners. Still, he could understand their feelings! But after all, the dead were dead and the prisoners were still men—no different than the guards in their inner needs and suffering. Thus there was no choice to be made between keepers and inmates. His heart reached out to everyone, to the prisoners in their fear and uncertainty and to the guards in their grief and anger.

His thoughts often went back to that day of violence. How strange it was, dearest listener! For I can tell you that in the sparkling processions of moments, filled with rifle shots and blaring sirens, the little man felt himself at peace; for one bristling moment he was entirely spent, every ounce of empathy was drained from him and spread throughout the prison.

Afterwards, one by one, virtually every official came to see him; each asked his advice, each shed his tears, and he helped all of them as best he could. Meanwhile word spread among the prisoners: the little guard's gun had not left his holster. Such things do not remain a secret for long and it was odd that none of the prison officials even mentioned it.

The response of the prisoners was different. When the prisoners heard the news they were finally won over; they finally came to realize that they loved this little man. In fact, it eventually became a tradition that every year his birthday would be celebrated in the cell of one inmate or another.

That last year it took place in the cell of a murderer; he was a man who had killed an elderly tramp and whose sentence was still being appealed. The celebration was merry. The prisoners found a little record player and the men danced with each other; a bit of beer had been smuggled in, jokes were told, and even a few gifts were given.

On the next day, all returned to the normal rounds of their lives, a routine which persisted until the prisoner in question heard that his last appeal had been rejected. The date of his execution was set and this guard of ours began to spend ever more time with this man who knew the day of his own death.

Now, can you imagine that, my friend?

To know the day when one will die; to know the time at which one will be no more; to recognize the hour, unchosen, imposed from without. Why, the horror of such knowledge far surpasses the sentence itself!

Immoral?

The sentence?

Drivel, I say! Why, one might as well condemn death itself for being immoral. Don't you agree, my Angel?

No! No! Not death itself, but the knowledge! To be forced to know! To know exactly the precise moment at which one will be cast into nothingness! The single point on the face of a watch, the split second at which the umbilical cord to all that surrounds one will be cut!

Look into my Lady's eyes, my friend, and you will see her pleasure!

Such is the ingenious character of the law. Death itself? A side issue, is it not my Love? Consider the interim and you will see what I mean. Just consider how each of time's divisions will taunt all that remains, and become an exquisite torture for what is left of the future. Consider if you will how each sound, each touch, taste and smell, will become nothing more than a reminder of that complete oblivion which will occur . . . then!

Don't think for a moment that the little guard didn't experience these thoughts. Even if he didn't formulate them quite in the way which I described, the little fellow could see the prisoner's face grow thin and hear his voice become dull; he could feel the tension in the warden's office and the anguish which permeated the warden's mind at having to carry out his first execution order.

Bah! But no matter! The little guard never spoke about such thoughts, either with the prisoner or with the warden. With both he did nothing other than listen; the criminal spoke of his upbringing and of his crimes, of his wife and of his love affairs, of food and of sports; the warden spoke about his father and made small talk.

Both did their best to keep the approaching day out of their minds. But, inevitably, it arrived and the hours started to strip themselves bare. Technically, it was the guard's day off. It was frightfully humid. When the guard left his house a moist sticky rain was falling and, by the time he had reached the prison, he was soaked to the skin.

He entered the warden's office immediately. Barely a word was exchanged, but the little fellow did not miss the warden's imploring look. When the guard entered the prisoner's cell the latter was already pecking away at his last meal. As soon as the guard sat down his eyes caught the signs of sweat which the prisoner's hands had left on the cell bars. The prisoner finished eating and an unusual silence took hold—a silence which gradually became even more oppressive. It weighed thickly in the air. To break the tension—without taking his eyes off the damp spots on the bars—the guard timidly began to speak with the same gentle compassion which he had always shown to the prisoner. For want of anything better, he told of how guilt was wracking the warden, how horrible too that this fine man should be compelled . . .

But then the guard abruptly shifted his gaze. With a presentiment of fear he noticed that the prisoner's face was changing. A look began to form, a look which absorbed the face; a force, an inexplicable fury seemed to be gathering momentum behind that look until suddenly the prisoner sprang from his chair and lunged at the guard. It was as if the guard were held fast by that look. For the criminal grabbed him, shook him and then smashed him frantically against the cell door.

The guard went for his gun, probably from instinct. Trembling in his fingers, it went off and fell to the floor. The prisoner backed away and the guard picked up the revolver. The prisoner came to his senses immediately, but offered no apology; the guard tried to speak, but the prisoner only turned his back on him. The guard haplessly left the cell and two hours later the prisoner was executed.

Nothing was the same after that. On that very day the little guard handed in his resignation. Within two weeks he had left the city, broken contact with the prisoners and the warden, and began to drink.

No, dearest friend! It wasn't the violence. True, never before had the guard been manhandled, never before had he been struck. Still this violence, the memory of the sound which his body made as it was thrown against the bars, was soon forgotten. The violence was explicable: anything could have caused it, the tension, the fear, the inappropriate reflections about the warden; it could have even been the poor quality of the prisoner's last meal.

No! It was something else, something far more intangible which affected the guard. It was the memory of the prisoner's look and the thought of the tears glistening in the warden's eyes.

Yes, my Lady! This was the same man who had made his pact with the living in their needs and anguish. Unfortunately, however, he was also the very man who would be haunted by the dead.

I have said it before: the little fellow was a decent man, a man who sought to comfort humanity. But the look of that prisoner, that living being who had been led to his death, seemed to call for vengeance; the little guard couldn't help but think of those poor devils in chains, behind bars—their frustration, the torpor in which they lived, the routine, the . . . And yet there were the warden's tears! There were those officials everywhere who so bravely carried the weight of those responsibilities which society had bestowed on them.

Somehow the little guard knew that a choice was necessary. But he didn't want to choose, he didn't even want to think about the choice. For, were he even to contemplate such a choice, his vision of humanity as an all-embracing entity would crumble; humanity would be cut in two.

The look and the tears! The conflict between them was unbearable. In the beginning the guard would dream of the look, he would wake up in a sweat and then, from the darkness, gradually the tears would take form and taunt him without respite into the early hours of the morning. Later, in the afternoon, the look would sparkle from the salt water droplets and often, in fact, he would astonish even himself at the horror which would overcome him while lingering somewhere or another. Yet the look and the tears gradually faded from his mind—only the images of a prisoner and an official remained.

The little fellow had never learned how to be partisan. And now he could not even choose between the living and the dead. For the living killed the dead, but the dead extracted the terror of remorse as payment. The tables turn. Who is the oppressor and who the oppressed? No easy question for one who has always seen suffering as suffering, for one who has always chosen not to choose!

Thus it was that the little guard found himself unable to resolve the dilemma which plagued him or relieve the tension which was slowly rotting away his existence. The decision which the future held in store was only a matter of time in coming; it was a decision the content of which is not so very difficult to surmise.

But I know my Lady! Ah! She would never allow so blatant a tragedy to occur when a more refined one exists as an alternative.

Oh! I can see you now my obscene Angel as you must have appeared to him then! Nude, your stomach distended like the stomachs of the starving. You probably drew his attention with a seductive gaze of sorrow in your eyes. Yes! You beckoned and he came forward, taking notice of your powerful arms, your disgusting legs, as all the while silence reigned.

I can see it all now! As he approaches you become ever uglier, but still he approaches. With no one to comfort him perhaps he will think that, through you, he will finally overcome the images of the warden and the prisoner. You appear humble, but then you give your toothless grin and finally he comes to see you as a madman's distortion. And then he must find an escape!

Mea culpa! Suffering stands before him—or wait, it may be oppression instead! But it's all the same! In that electric instant he will think; the prisoner suffered, the warden suffered, both suffered—but lo!! I suffer more than either!

And I can see my Lady's eyes shine with joy! Inward he turns! Away with the guilt of inaction! Away with the terror of choice! Away with a humanity which no one can define!

Then the little guard will withdraw from the world; he will become the type of ascetic who cultivates his inner anguish. He will come to believe that there is no one who can possibly understand the sorrow which he has seen, the sorrow which he has borne. He will shut his eyes and his heart will grow hard until, at last, he will become what he has always sought to be; the saint, the man who refuses to choose from amongst men, the unknown marytr to whom my Lady will doubtless give her blessing.

All of it is true, my friend! As true, I tell you, as if you yourself had put a mirror up to his soul! For, you see, in a manner of speaking, this is just what I did as I sat beside him on that evening when I listened to his story.

He came here often. Sitting quietly, he would shift his gaze from the ceiling to the candle flickering brightly on the table. Whenever we sat together a layer of cigarette smoke surrounded him as he drank. And, my God, how he drank! He would always lay a twenty dollar bill on the counter and drink steadily until not a cent remained. He never drank too fast nor too slowly; it was a pleasure to watch!

On the night he told his tale the little fellow's eyes never left his glass until, suddenly, he broke off his story. Then, with blood-shot eyes, he stared at me and, with his index finger stuck in my chest, he exclaimed in a voice loud enough for everyone to hear that I was a caricature of the devil! Can you imagine that?

In an instant he was gone and I didn't see him again for quite some time although I heard from a third party that he had married a fifty year old spinster, that they had decided to adopt children, and that he had taken a job selling insurance. The last time I saw him I was sitting on a bench in a tiny park on a hazy, muggy afternoon. He was taking his family for a walk, and the little fellow seemed lost in thought, paying no heed to his jabbering wife who was riveted to his arm. The children were walking glumly in front of them and I had the distinct impression that they didn't like their father very much—which is really a pity since he was always so fond of children. I vaguely remember that I nodded to him as they passed, but that he didn't so much as lift his hat in return.

Part Two

I

SO, you see that there are tales in which a character can simply drift through his existence. These are wonderful tales! Tales in which action takes the form of inaction and dreams about the future are replaced by illusions about the present. In stories such as these, life becomes a fixed destiny, an iron fate over which one has no control. These are the tales which my Lady adores for, in these stories, the world can only become what it already is. Yes! In these tales, one looks to humanity—and one is left alone, resigned and without hope; in such stories, a man quivers in his inwardness and the world is left to run its course uninterrupted.

And yet, how one longs for the unexpected—for the moment which will pry one loose from one's destiny! Even here, in this very café . . . If only I could express the emotion which welled up in my heart as *she* approached my table! How different the night became! How this banal little café was transformed!

No! The effects of such an encounter cannot be minimized. You see, particularly in a place like this, one is accustomed to a succession of evenings in which each becomes nothing more than an extension of those which have preceded it.

Come to think of it, perhaps it is even a part of the café's attraction! In the continuum of destiny, the thought of what is yet to come—what might come—is made that much more intense! The anticipation becomes that much more forceful, the dream of the unexpected that much more stark!

Yes, it's true! As I look around me there's not a patron who does not anticipate the unexpected. An unclaimed relic of the past, an inkling of the future! Anything will do, so long as one can finally be tossed into a new realm, a dynamic realm, a realm of excitement for which one never has to pay a price.

What a world! A nether-world, to be experienced without reflection or activity. Isn't that what we await, my Lady?

And that was just the world which leapt to my eyes as I gazed at her. Oh, it had been years since I had seen her last—eons, it seemed! Why, I would swear that a day never passed in which I didn't think of her, and . . .

All right, my Darling! Perhaps one day, eh?

Ha! But really, I do sometimes shudder at your cynicism!

Just so long as *you* don't get the wrong idea, my friend! For I tell you that, in my own way, I loved her once—albeit from afar! But that's not quite true, for we would often talk long into the night and we would exchange little presents as well. Oh! How modest my desires were!

Do you remember that little fat gentleman whom I pointed out earlier? Take another look at him. Do you see the tiepin that he's wearing? Well, that trinket once belonged to me—a generous gift from the woman in question.

But hard times abound! What a state of affairs . . . and one speaks of casting pearls before swine!

The confession must be made, my lustful Angel! Her tale must be told, and you should not be taken aback! There is no cause for jealousy. Still, when I think of her face. Such a beautiful, oval, expressive face . . . But then, I can remember that face during another time: when it was disjointed and drawn, when the eyelids were heavily closed. I see that face, that body, lying in a room not much larger than a closet; the hands of a corpse falling off a cot, touching the floor, with the tracks jutting out of an arm like small hills on a flat horizon. The room was cheap and uncluttered, very different from the other place, with its knickknacks strewn all around and the grand piano sitting squarely in the middle of an immense living room.

But, of course, by then the piano was gone too; it had been sold to a rather morose gentleman who wished to start taking lessons for some obscure reason. Those evenings which led up to the sale were horrifying! I would come to her, even though I could do nothing more than sit and watch the sweat pour from her skin, and taste the vomit on her tongue as the drops of mucus from her nose ran over her lips. Yes, I would stare at her in her languor, as her heavy fingers occasionally scratched one part of her body or another, while her mouth hung open like a gaping wound.

There was little to say. The evil which simultaneously repulsed and attracted me always seemed to be perched where it could spy on my words. Always it sought to pull me in from the outside, until finally she and I became opposing partners in a conspiracy against . . .

Oh, my Lady! Don't glare at me so! There's no need for jealousy—you silly thing! I had to go to her! What else could I do? Rest assured though, I hated every second which I spent with her! Yet she would plead with me to come and, besides, you know how helpful I can be in such situations. So please, don't . . .

What's that, my friend?

You want to know how I met her?

A most appropriate question! Well, I must confess that it was a simple, straightforward encounter. You see, I had decided to go to the theater and her performance had positively thrilled me. Afterwards, I waited outside the stage entrance. Of course, there were others waiting for autographs, but I needn't tell you —most worldly fellow that you are!—of what breed they were. What I remember best is that they all giggled! And how I detest those creatures who giggle! You can imagine how badly I wanted to meet her since I put up with being surrounded by such parochial company. In spite of it all, I maintained my composure and when she emerged—without having to say a word—she immediately noticed my presence.

In this way, our—how shall I say?—association began. That very night we went for coffee and spoke of the loftiest subjects. The evening took on a peculiar brilliance; a distinctness, no doubt a product of the extreme cold, accentuated every object. The sidewalk glowed and streetlights seemed to bounce off the iron gratings that were installed to protect the smaller boutiques.

A criss-cross of light hounded our vision. Even in the coffee shop it broke through the large windows and illuminated the faces of the two couples who were sitting in the booth opposite us. They said nothing. Again and again we looked over at them, held fast as in a *nature morte*—the very appropriate French term for what we call a still life. Then, finally, we saw an expression change slightly. One of the boys sniggered, almost to himself, and the silence was broken.

Suddenly, a wave of sadness overcame us. In a melancholy tone I asked what had led her to become an actress. She smiled, and in a low voice said that, when she was a little girl, her grandmother had told her of a man she had met abroad many years ago. The old woman had told her that he was an extraordinary man. Yes, that he was a man of great wisdom who explained to her that when one looks to art, one discovers both oppression and those needs which form the truth that lies in the hope for a new world.

For a while her grandmother thought that she was in love with this fellow. But apparently the old woman never took up either the romance or the quest. During the following year she married a sensible farmer and settled down in a small town somewhere in the midwest. There she raised her children and later watched her family grow apart.

The little actress told me that the old woman regretted her choice until the day of her death. My acquaintance was still a child when she swore not to make the same mistake that her grandmother had made.

Yet while the actress was speaking of her grandmother, of truth and hope, I couldn't help thinking of the audience: poor little men roasting in their suits and ties, their overdressed and garrulous wives, and the young, with their expressions of profundity, wearing neatly clipped beards and faded dungarees. All of them waited patiently in the theater with the romanesque ceiling; all of them waited to watch this genius perform.

And a genius she was! Every critic said so! During her performances a wonderful tension would be manifested. One part of her body would complement another in perfect harmony while each clear tone brought forth a mystery. Yes, she almost seemed to disappear behind the lines which she recited. At a given point, in fact, she would vanish like an apparition at sunrise and in the audience's anticipation of her reemergence, they would find themselves seduced: then they would be hers.

I saw her when she played a classic role: that of a dear lady of exquisite manners—if rather primitive desires—who finds herself somehow drawn to her own brother-in-law. A woman, reared in the culture of a South long gone, stands face to face with her relation, a crude barbarian male who is to symbolize the new age. She is an anachronism, like the beautiful world to which she feels herself bound. This is a world which she can never relinquish and so she begins to recreate it for herself in her fantasies. A squalid life, without mansions, slaves or etiquette, comes into conflict with her innate delicacy. Her brother-in-law is bothered by her affectations. But these feelings change once he learns of her rather interesting sexual past—a past which her delicate sensibility naturally refuses to allow her to accept. For her sexuality is bound to her loneliness and, of course, everyone strives to overcome his isolation. But her brother-in-law understands none of this, particularly when he hears of her attempted seduction of a delivery boy. All respect for her is shattered—which is no doubt why he rapes this woman growing old while his wife is in the hospital having his baby.

A marvelous story! A wonderful theme! But that's not all! Because of her previous fantasies—which unfortunately always appeared to others as lies—no one believes her regarding what took place. Two options are left open—as in any respectable work of this genre—suicide or madness. Thus, by the play's end, we find her being led away to an asylum while the ugly unfeeling world goes on as before.

What a work I tell you! One seemed to sense the playwright; the master's presence seemed to fill the vacuum of the hall. Sitting there, I swallowed it all; every gesture, every nuance struck me as profoundly moving. But, thinking about it in the lobby, I realized that it was all because of her.

Yes, it was she! She, the liar! Truly it was she alone who brought my emotions to a fever's pitch. It was nothing other than she—*the actress as liar*—behind whose lips the words were being cajoled, cursed and then manipulated, and all to one end.

When this occurred to me . . . Oh, you can just imagine how I was able to appreciate once again the striving of the words, the tension of the ideas, the thrust of the emotions until their final apocalypse in the applause.

I must say that in spite of this wave of sadness, we did spend a very nice evening together. Still—if I remember correctly—she did grow a bit pale when I tactfully mentioned my impressions of the play.

At that point, she hastily said that she had to leave. But she didn't leave. Instead she described how during one of her soliloquies her eye fastened on a mask hanging backstage. It was a devil's mask with a mocking smile! How vile it looked! How horrible its features!

Oh! I can see my Lady's being filling that mask! I can see my Angel leading the eye of this young woman to one of the few empty seats in the house. Yes! I can see my Lady projecting the image of one empty seat turning to two, two turning to three, three to four, four to five, until finally the whole house is empty.

I looked into this young woman's eyes and I could see her standing alone with what she sought to express. All her ideals grew hollow, and it was then that I saw doubt erupt in this young woman's heart.

Suddenly, however, she shook her head. Once again she got up to leave. This time she excused herself by saying that there was to be a party the following night and that she had to get to bed early. Over her polite protests, there and then, I immediately agreed to escort her.

Oh! And the party! It was simply divine! The walls were

lined with mirrors, and the food was superb: a truly resplendent buffet which stretched from one end of the room to the other. Guests packed the large apartment and the company was quite convivial. Loud music blared from the finest speakers and there was dancing everywhere. Liquor flowed and there was cocaine for everyone.

Occasionally one would see a couple *tête à tête*, but mostly small groups would gather, disperse, and then form anew. Wherever one looked there was movement, on-going, never-ending movement, even in the corner where a good-looking fellow was furiously scribbling his thoughts on a napkin.

And those mirrors! I remember turning and seeing my little actress staring into one of them. My Lady's face flashed before her, and then the mask—that terrible mask of cynicism and despair.

How my Darling must have laughed! Again the vision of hopelessness! Again the empty theater! Again a distorted truth!

I could see my little actress clench her fists. I could see how she longed to shatter that mirror—but she did nothing, and the moment was gone. It was then that her eye fell upon that fellow sitting in the corner writing on a napkin—it was then that she took him as a lover.

And I stood back and watched her walk over to him. From the mirrors, smiling faces sought out my eyes. The ladies were so charming and they always put their hands on the arms of the men to whom they were speaking. And the gentlemen, they were so inoffensive—so helpful and kind—that I believed my little actress when she told me later that these were the types who would be able to exist under any regime.

Oh, it's true! I was never of their sort! I was always a man apart. But who was I to dispute my little actress's wisdom? Slightly cultured, sufficiently skeptical while engaging to a fault, all of them most certainly would find themselves at home in a world . . .

—No! I do not care to accompany you! Besides, there's already someone in the bathroom!

—What's that, you say?

—Why, you miserable little wretch! I have a good mind to...

The little fat one again! Oh, he knew that I wouldn't agree. He saw that I was in the middle of a story. But, like a fool, he chooses to persist in his belief that a single experience will determine a manifold future.

Confidentially though, I have the feeling that he actually came to see me out of guilt. For the little fat one is a man who simply accepts his world. He is not a man to bother with truth, and so he always seeks to do penance.

Now I ask you, what better way to do penance than to seek out a rejection? Well, perhaps there are other ways. But it all depends on how one determines and then defines his guilt. My little actress? She would also find her way.

All this, however, makes me think of a tale which she once told me. Did you know that in ancient times—in Babylonia, I believe she said—there was a custom according to which every woman was supposed to prostitute herself in the temple on the night before her marriage?

Now, consider if you will a timid little country peasant whose soft eyes manifest her purity. She has had little education and so the thought of the approaching day fills her with a mixture of fear and awe. She knows nothing of the temple or the city; her life has been circumscribed within a small village in which her family has dwelled for generations. She and her fiancé have known each other since they were children. She loves him and her family as well; she has always felt herself content enough to fall asleep without fearing her dreams.

But then, one day, her calm is broken. The world intervenes. She is summoned to the city, to the teeming metropolis, in the middle of which stands the temple. With due humility she allows herself to be led inside. She has already been informed of her duties and she has made her sacrifices. Agonizingly, she stares at the priest who touches her breast as he disrobes her. Then she is led into a huge hall, adorned with statues, where a few other women are sitting on a shiny floor.

After a while the men are let in—the worshippers. A brute

approaches. Let us imagine that he is a soldier—a huge hairy monster of a man, wounded in battle and perhaps missing an eye or an ear, with a scar or two. With an appraising look he surveys her body and finds it pleasing. Horror rips through her like a spear and yet inwardly—in some strange and perverse fashion—she is proud and almost happy as well.

But then gripping her arm, the warrior drags her off to an empty corner. Throwing her roughly on the ground, he rips off her clothing with one hand while, with the other, he pulls her hair in such a way that she will be forced to watch everything. Slowly he lowers himself on top of her. He grabs and squeezes her flesh, squeezes for what must seem like an eternity to a woman who has known only gentleness.

When she chances to open her eyes, she sees only his back and the marks which her nails have left. He stands naked, with a triumphant smile on his lips. Only then is she overcome by shame.

Why had she obeyed so passively? Why had she done what had been asked of her? Why did she act for this malformed giant's pleasure? What was the cowardly joy, that deceitful pride which she had experienced? What type of liar had she become?

All those questions take no more than a second to ask, and then she moans—as she will moan again and again in the course of that day. Yes, in such moans horror and ecstasy are reconciled as the rack turns into a confessional. Always, along with the moan, the thoughts return—the questions. Another warrior approaches her, and then still another, until that tender tissue between her legs becomes so sore that the thought of the bruises it has yet to receive melts from her consciousness—along with her thoughts, her questions—leaving only a grotesque sanctity which she feels will be irrevocably hers and hers alone.

The hours pass and finally it comes to an end. Only the priest is left. But our country girl has grown a little wiser; she already knows what her last sacrifice will entail. The priest pushes her to her knees in front of him and . . . Well, the god is quite satisfied, or so the priest tells her as he flings her a rag to wipe her face. She is free to leave. Suddenly, however, as he turns his back, to register her disgust, to show her hatred, she spits on the ground.

She would never have even contemplated such a thing before! Sacrilege! The priest turns his head, walks back towards her, looks at the small pool of saliva, slaps her across the face with the back of his hand—and grins. The priest shakes his head as if thinking to himself: so very foolish, so very useless. Holding her jaw, she sees that the priest can afford to grin, that he is right; she realizes that the action was nothing but a gratuitous gesture—it was too small, too isolated, and it had come too late.

During her journey home, she longs for her fiancé. In him the world's ugliness will be extinguished. In him—through him—she will exorcise the thought of those actions which she never undertook, those questions which she never asked. Yet, when she finally sees him, when she tries to speak, there is not a word which she can say. For these moments of torment have already become fused into a passion, and the passion has already become a penance. Thinking about this man with whom she will spend her life, she finds him decent, sensitive—there is nothing for him to do, nothing which he can give.

Even during the ceremony, the moments cling to her, become part of her, no different than the hair which lies matted in knots on her head—a part of her which grows ever more powerful with each minute, and which she knows she will never be able to express until the others . . . So, at last, she comprehends that eventually she will come to think about this passion as little as about her nails and, strange as it may seem, as soon as she realizes this, she instinctively knows that she will grow old quickly.

A man such as myself, of course, stands above the darkness of guilt, age and death. But those others! Those who embrace the darkness like a forgotten vision, those are the ones!

Ah yes! Like the bat, they are drawn to darkness—and this darkness burns! Let me tell you that it burns right through one's insides; a turbulence explodes the sensibility and always this darkness—either as terror or as melancholy—is recalled as one is pushed ever closer to the outer edges of chaos.

Just so with my little actress! Once doubt had penetrated her heart, terror seized her mind. Ach! She was treated shabbily, I dare say abused, both by her audience and her lover. The audience is always fickle, that we know. But her lover . . . Yet, this is not to imply that the fellow was either particularly inconsiderate or intentionally malicious. There are many people who have these faults—and they can be handled. But a man such as he . . .

No! No! What she couldn't comprehend, what she wished to explain, what had turned him into an object of hatred, was the way he seemed to mimic what she wished to express through her art.

So very sincere! So very supportive! So very hopeful! He saw her in her misery. But what did he do? He told her to be strong! He saw her in her doubt and guilt. What did he do? He told her to search her imagination and look to her talent! He told her to forget the doubt, forget the guilt, forget the audience and forget the world! Oh! And she tried! But then . . .

— Get away from me! Waitress! Where the devil are you?

— Get this vicious animal away from my foot!

— My word!

— Tell your superior that I'll sue if he doesn't keep this creature chained! See if I won't! I assure you that I have friends in the highest places and that I'll . . .

— Ah! There.

— Why, that's very nice of you!

— Yes, I think another drink would calm me down a bit.

— Now! Now! You needn't apologize! I know that a woman of your refinement would never approve of someone owning such a dangerous pet!

— Oh! A smile from you soothes all . . . But please don't forget about the drink. Another double *crème de menthe*, eh?

You really must excuse me, dearest friend. You see, whenever I come in here that damned poodle feels called upon to cuddle at my leg. And how I detest small dogs!

The very idea! The manager of an establishment such as this owning a toy poodle! He probably bought a black one to match his soul!

Well, to return to my little actress, I couldn't help noticing how much older she had become, how much more severe in her manner. To be sure, she looked better than when I saw her last, but that says very little. Indeed, it was as if the years which we spent apart had been engraved on her face. Always it would be her face! And, as I looked at her, quietly and yet inflexibly she drew me back in time to a particular night which she once spent with this fellow.

This was the night in which she told him of the mask, of the audience, and of the doubt growing inside her. The words flowed from her lips, but his hands roamed up her thighs. They moved to her breasts and to her face and the words seemed to recoil in her mind as he led her to the bedroom. Dreamily she told of how she had wanted him to enter her. But a dull echo of those words seemed to remain, and so he murmured with a sigh that perhaps they should wait a bit longer. As she described it, the sheets were already wet with perspiration when they finally started to move: rhythmically, slowly at first and then faster, over and over again, in what she could only recall as a singular monotony.

The words were forgotten. She felt at peace.

So who ever said that a night's pleasure depends upon the act alone? Why, I myself have never been able to determine the intrinsic value of sex. In fact, the matter has troubled me for quite some time although I admit that of late my interest in the question has diminished considerably. Now there are only the moments after in which the cigarettes are lit and the knowing looks exchanged. Looks which . . .

Oh, her lover meant well! Be assured of that, my friend! He told her that he loved her. He spoke of the inspiration which she gave him. He swore that he needed her, that he needed her talent for his own. And yet, long afterwards, all that she could remember was that singular monotony and the loss of those words. . . .

But then, suddenly, she smiled her wonderful smile: "a pimp in a pin-striped suit."

She had always tried to describe him to others and—after a time—even to conjure him up to herself. She had always failed, but now . . . I saw her swell with pride as she proceeded to embellish her creation: a pimp on a stool speaking of genius, fingering his pipe with one hand and stroking her knee with the other. A panderer of illusions and abstract hope!

Once again—or maybe for the first time—she felt herself an artist. And yet this latent image must have clung to her like a leech during those years in which she was desperately trying to give that amorphous memory a recognizable form.

To structure this horrible content through words! To shape it by cognition! . . .

You're right, my friend. It's not much of an image when you think about it. Nevertheless, it helped provide her with still another insight into that extraordinary existence which she had experienced. So don't be too quick in your judgments for, believe me, you still know very little about her.

II

How little even I know about her! Dear God! When I think that she should have become what she became! Why, a chill runs down my spine!

If one only knew why!

Yes, it's true! Everyone wants to be a star. The competition is fierce, the pressure is intense and continuous. And yet there are those who triumph over their competitors and others who can withstand the pressure—even my little actress withstood the competition and the pressure for the longest time.

I remember discussing her plight with the fellow who had murdered his grandfather. His response was: "Look to others."

I still don't fully understand what he meant. But I do have an idea! For somehow it seems that it is the company that one keeps which shapes both an individual's view of the world and of himself.

And hers was an exclusive company! The burden which they bore was awesome—for it was their responsibility to preserve culture. They were the visible symbols of that industry which decided what the mass should see, read and enjoy. But that's not all! For culture dare not stand still! Thus it is this group which must also remain *avant*—always *avant!*

Now, I guess that once experiencing life as a gay whirl was *de rigueur* for those who counted. But from what I have seen, it seems that it has been quite some time since the privileged have chosen to view themselves as such. Especially if one believes what one reads, it becomes clear that their social lives are always defined by private tragedies.

After all, everything is permitted to the rich and famous. Yet, how tragic it is to be permitted everything! And then too, the stage for their private dramas is the entire world! Oh, the tragedy of the limelight! The intrusions of reporters! The endless flights from one place to another! Never a moment of simple peace!

And this company of hers was not to be outdone!

So doesn't it make sense that, even among themselves, they should view their lives as being endowed with a kind of aura? Is it any wonder that they should exaggerate their problems a bit—that they should learn to despair?

You see, the search for fashion never ends—and so, even despair can become fashionable. Besides, what catches the public's eye better than despair? And this despair even serves a purpose! Why, it becomes clear to the most indigent fool that everyone suffers. Thus, there is no reason why a guilt-ridden, hopeless despair shouldn't become the order of the day!

And yet, to meet the requirements of this crisis of conscience, these people must substitute existential concerns for material problems—which, after all, do not plague them in the least. A taste of despair, of doubt, or anguish, is a healthy thing! And then too, when the experience becomes dull there is always that wealth which is held in reserve.

Of course, I would imagine that most of the little actress's friends were aware of the manner in which their despair was circumscribed. But apparently she was not.

Now, now! My Lady! No need to throw a tantrum! I am not

insensitive! Why, I even like the rich! I am merely trying to make a point! One must look to the cultural milieu—that's what I say!

Her lover? He was little more than a carcass in which she could see that complex of images which plagued her: a mask perpetually changing its features, the emptiness of a theater, and the failings of the audience.

Indeed, it was particularly when she looked into his eyes that she saw the failings of the audience. And it made sense—for he was them! In truth, he was them! Even before she had ever met him, she had seen him a thousand times in a hundred different theaters—only, then, she hadn't noticed. They were interchangeable—he and each member of the audience, each believing himself to be unique, each no different from the rest.

These were the thoughts which received expression on the night of her last performance before a nearly empty theater. I remember her saying: Before the curtain is raised, when the theater lights still glare, doesn't each look out at the rest and think that he sees the world in its entirety? Doesn't each maintain the illusion that he is unique? Doesn't each need the proof necessary to make his belief a conviction? Of course, no one will *do* anything to manifest his singularity! Instead each will wait for me to give him the experience which will separate him from that fool shuffling in his seat to the right and that woman fiddling with her rings on the left.

She looked to me then and there was nothing to say. She had come to understand her function; that her job was to convince every one of them that he had achieved what in fact he hadn't achieved at all. I realized that she understood; that, while seeking to express what she subjectively believed was a higher truth, she had betrayed herself and her audience as well.

But enough! When I saw her last, I could only think of her then—back when the first transition was just beginning.

After the performances she would remain in the theater amid the throng of directors, actors, technicians, playwrights, and parts of an everchanging audience. She could not articulate her disgust to those around her, or that anguished doubt which was growing within her. Each was withdrawn into himself and so, when she approached, when she began to stutter, they all chided her gently, or patted her shoulder warmly, or maintained that it was time for a little lift.

Alone with her anguish, it was almost as if this emotion was taking the place of those to whom she could not speak. Anguish drew her close. Indeed, she felt its tug with that same mixture of wonder and fear which a little boy feels when he is playing in the tide.

Oh, my Lady! If only you could have been there! It was terrifying to watch her rehearse. She would take hold of her script boldly; inwardly, however, she would back away as if that bundle of papers had turned into a snarling predator. Each night was the same, although she felt her incapacity growing, until finally her anguish devoured her.

In the beginning she would shudder and this elusive anguish would fade—only to be called back again. In between, she would turn to her lover. But he could offer her nothing—and she would become melancholic. Thus, although as yet she did not know much about the larger world outside the theater, she decided to flee.

Hmmph! To flee from him, from her anguish, from her melancholy. They were all completely interwoven in her mind.

Still, such a flight takes some time; such a decision is rarely accomplished in one stroke. Yet, once this anguished doubt had permeated her work the end was already in sight. On the stage, in the audience, her impotence became ever more apparent. It slowly became clear that she was no longer the same sorceress who cast her spells at will. Instead she emerged as a woman, someone the same as they themselves—truly the same as they themselves—and, once this became evident, their response was assured. That special mode of communication which had once presented itself to her naturally, in those creaking seats and hushed coughs, gradually began to slip away. Though stripped of her aura, she would still look out from the glaring lights into the blackness for her acclaim, an acclaim which was no longer forthcoming.

Finally the night came. There was no applause when the curtain went down. The audience was sullen as it streamed to the doors and not one critic came to her dressing room. The morning papers praised the play, but mercilessly attacked her performance. "Uninspired!" "Amateurish!" "Hesitant!" "Dull!"—those were the words which they used to describe her.

Ah! She wanted not to care! She tried desperately to feign indifference! But, under my Lady's watchful gaze, this young woman's inner despair drew her towards the abyss—and she felt as if there were nothing she could do to counteract its pull.

Again and again, she thought of the devil's mask with the fool's grin. She thought of the empty seats . . . At her next performance there were plenty of empty seats; the next play in which she agreed to act closed after two nights.

If only you could have seen her . . . She redoubled her efforts . . . More rehearsals and then still more . . . But she would forget her lines; then she would change her pose and her palms would become moist as she prepared her muscles for that gesture which never came. Again and again, she would begin her lines only to halt as the image of a suffering audience overcame her. Always there was the thought of the silence, of the repressed hisses, of the critic's snide remarks, and her own inadequacy, until finally the director would suggest that it might be wiser to start fresh in the morning.

Then, however, the night would really begin! Then we would go to a club and try to dull that persistent ache inside her with a quart of gin. But often liquor wouldn't do the trick. So, for those times, we would find ourselves a charming young lady, or gentleman, who would provide a bit of mindless diversion after escorting us home.

Yet, in time, even this no longer sufficed. The evenings became longer—like the days. She went to her friends. Once they had been so comforting, so nice—she couldn't even imagine them as anything but comforting or nice. But she learned; when they spoke to her it was in brusque tones: no gentleness, no tact, no parts. And during those days she also learned how to wait—for agents, for directors, even for publicity men. There was a time when she could walk into an office and all the doors would fly open. But after a fiasco or two . . .

She stared at the doors.

Tell me, my friend, do you know what it is like to stare at a door? To count the grains in the wood? To peer into those concentric circles for hours on end?

Yes! She stared at those doors and finally allowed the abyss to engulf her.

I was with her when she made her first purchase. In fact, I even introduced her to the fellow from whom she bought the drugs.

Please! Your protests are superfluous. If it wouldn't have been me, it would most assuredly have been someone else. At least my dealer was reliable. At least I remained with her when she started to grow numb—and yet . . .

Oh, dearest listener! On that evening in which she sat across from me, she swore that, beyond her numbness, she was always conscious of a waking dream—and I have no cause to doubt her! Even when she was well along her path, I'm sure that she was able to experience a meager fantasy—a vague fantasy of liberation—which transcended the domination of those needles which always lay uncovered in her drawer.

It's true! This fantasy was cut off from both action and the world. In fact, at her depths there was never even a question of action—or choice. Action no longer existed, choice no longer existed, her colleagues no longer existed, the audiences no longer existed! No! Nothing existed any longer, for it was as if all of history had become compressed into the fluid which bobbed up and down the needle.

Omnivorous, the needles drew in every bit of reality. But this is precisely the point! It was every part of the reality which she despised, the reality from which fantasy breaks free! To be sure, hers was a fantasy without content—only a semblance of the full force which lies in the imagination—but yet, a semblance it remained, a semblance which she somehow managed to preserve.

How hard it must have been to preserve even that! Only for seconds at a time would this vague fantasy surface and then—

with a hush!—it would be gone. Yet, it was with wonder that she experienced it silently stalking beyond that continuum of terror which her life had become.

No, she never lost this either! She managed to retain that extraordinary sense of wonder by which she knew that it was she—she herself—who was moving along this path which she had chosen: a path which nothing except frustration, illusion, doubt, and despair had led her to follow.

And, my Lady, let me assure you that I was always watching! Oh, it might have been from a distance, but such an excursion was one which a . . . a . . . Ah! I know! . . a caricature of the devil could not afford to miss. Yes, indeed! I was always there even when she didn't see me and I didn't see her.

She would walk and, with each step on any street, I would feel her moving ever further into the gray shadings of the city's center. In the beginning she walked without seeing anything. The world vanished from her gaze for she felt that she had been expelled from amongst us.

Yes, like Cain, she felt compelled to wander in a phantasmagoria devoid of both mercy and shame. But, even in the haze, money had to be made—and there were few marketable skills which she possessed. She made her choice without hesitation. With each trick that she turned a fix could be bought: a fix through which she could feel herself akin to a bird that seemingly glides through the air without movement, its wings barely ruffled by the wind. Softly, almost blissfully, she felt herself carried away and yet, every now and then, her eyes would open and she would look back to the street.

In flashes, in clumps, she came to see everything. Yes, everything! From the poor in their undershirts sitting on the stoops, with open cans of beer in their hands and the drops of the contents dribbling down their chins, to the potbellied men with the silver mustaches strolling down very different avenues with engraved briefcases clenched in their fists. She saw working girls by day, gazing with romantic longing into the display windows, and hawkers by night who had nothing to sell but junk. She saw rats as long as a man's arm and streets which sparkled as if they had been inlaid with diamonds. She saw everything: a hundred thousand crisscrossing impressions—a hurricane of contradictory facts. Initially, she found it impossible to make sense of them. They seemed isolated like disparate themes—but then, she still retained a mode of thinking which was popular in what was once her little world; she had never learned to construct an idea based upon the world as it functioned.

Slowly, however, she began to try. She began to concentrate on what she saw as she walked. She walked alone; a prostitute is never bothered. She started to chain smoke and one cigarette replaced another as if in harmony with the dull monotony of her footsteps. Each night would take her to a different part of the city, but always she would return to the same park, to the same stone embankment from which on clear nights she could get a view of the stars lingering over a vast expansion bridge. When she was alone her loneliness was often exacerbated by the sounds of lovers in the bushes or the drone of the police car which patrolled the park after dusk.

There was nothing special about the night in which the second transition began. A trick or two and then her usual walk. On that night, however, as she sat on her embankment with a cigarette in her mouth and a match in her hand waiting to be struck, she suddenly started to shake, to shudder with such intensity that the cigarette fell from her lips. Every muscle, every nerve, felt itself contort with all the liberating horror of a negation—a total negation, complete and full.

She said that she got to her feet with a stagger although she was unable to explain how she made it home. She swore to me, however, that these were not simply the symptoms of withdrawal—those were to come later.

By the time she had returned to her apartment the fit had passed. But even then, the thought of its violence consumed her. Once inside, she locked the door. Two loaves of bread lay on the cupboard alongside a bottle of gin. In her icebox there was only some milk, a bar of butter, and some jam; a half-full jar of coffee and a bowl of sugar stood on the table.

Days passed before she left her apartment. Finally she was

to achieve her pinnacle of anguish. At first the pain gripped her to the point where she could barely utter a sound. Then she began talking to herself. But the words sounded alien, so she started playing the few records that she owned. She played them again and again, particularly Beethoven's Fifth Symphony.

Oh, my Lady! I swear to you that her description of this piece almost made the tale of her lover seem worthwhile. Feverishly, she told of how she had experienced the flutes as in a dream. Instinctively, she allied herself with the horns and supported them—against the rest of the orchestra—for those notes which could comprise their solos. And then she waited with the expectancy of a child for that moment of suspense which affords the transition to the last movement once the string trio has ended.

She would listen to this final movement innumerable times! Spellbound, she felt the music's intensification of strength and, towards the close, its decline. But the first close was always a lie and ultimately the music came to be saved from that sham ending so that once again, free and fresh, a crescendo arose with a force and vigor which seemed to propel the music's promise through the phonograph and into the world itself.

When she could stand no more she tried to read. She had always loved Shakespeare and so she sought to immerse herself in him—at least to the extent which her situation allowed. Even during the most terrible moments, however, the works remained in her thoughts and, as the last bits of white powder were used up, one character began to fade into another, mixing with her vomit, chills, and fear.

Just try to imagine it, my Darling! Falstaff, his words turning into those of the beleaguered Lear and the remorseful Othello. The cynical wisdom of all the Fools catching those screams which erupted from her own throat.

And you had better believe that there were screams! An avalanche of screams that were seconded by Macbeth's bride. Blood flowed before my little actress's eyes, and—think of it!—she saw Hamlet's corpse, her own foot grinding into his face. Yes, she was a participant in the tragedy, and she felt Richard's amused gaze pricking her skin as the years of the transition began to dissolve.

Richard! . . "A horse! A horse! . ."

"Very well, you son of a bitch," she must have thought. "Very well, villain! You shall have your horse! What the poet has denied you I will grant to your disciple who is no less a villain than you! Yes! Now you will have your disciple who will say, in the same tone as you yourself, that 'I have set my life upon a cast, and I will stand the hazard of the die.' "

But then she wailed! To the emptiness of the room, she cried that she was not even a villain! Oh, were she only a villain, even for a moment! But she could only see herself in the glow of humanity's refuse and suddenly she knew that a villain was the lowest of creatures only to the mighty. She had learned that there was something lower, much lower, and that now it was time for those gods to stand up for the bastards they had spawned!

She remembered: an old man getting on a bus. She remembered; she had been struck with the thought of what a marvelous sculpture the man's head would make. He had taken off his hat and his skull was shining like a black planet. Perfect! The interconnection of those minute patches of skin which were bound by the tiniest lines.

Yes, she remembered: beauty had hung there within reach of the inner eyes of her mind. Dignity glimmered. But then she saw the unshaven cheeks, the cut and the dried blood on his lips, the tear in the hat which he held between his hands. Suddenly all the beauty, all the dignity, was crushed like his nose which still carried scars from the beatings he had received.

Once again, the landscape appeared before her—workers, thinkers, panderers and bureaucrats. Each was immune to the unseen wounds of the rest and the smiles of the masters. She looked at them and saw well fed slaves—slaves to the regimen of production, consumption, work and sleep. They were not their own, as little as she was her own.

The agonizing doubt within her and the melancholy which she showed to the world gradually started to perish. She was sucked deeper, ever deeper, into the crowd. And it was then, in an open moment in which reason and revelation merged, that she finally understood. The world was not as they said it was: each an actor playing his role for an audience, one compensating the other! In the needle's eye of the crowd, she understood that there are those who receive no remuneration whatsoever! That the *role* is of no consequence but that, instead, it is the *context* in which the role is played that matters! At last she came to see that there are those who receive nothing, nothing at all, not even a horse—let alone some applause.

She remembered. Every now and then she indifferently thought of what could be done for them, what could be done to uplift them, what could be done to alleviate their poverty, to bring them out of their misery. But suddenly she understood. Angrily, she cried: who said "Give a beggar a horse and you have a tyrant!" Who said that? The idiot! The masters know better! They know that all that results from such a gift is—not a tyrant!—but only that very same beggar plus a horse!

No! No horses! No gifts! No charity! No wages! Nothing should be given! Kindness is too cheap! She would help them take their horses! She would help them take their world and their truth as well—take it from those who thought they owned the future and its truth with the same complacency that they owned the present.

But the crowd was not theirs! The bastards would stand up for themselves! She would go to them! She would go to those who would accept no gifts, who would abolish gifts as they sought to reap the fruits of what they themselves had sown. It was to them that she would go! To those who would take whole what the masters would only give out piecemeal! She would go to them, the actual producers, who could still understand that they remained on the outside. She would go to them, she would tell them of her experiences, of the audiences and the streets! She would . . .

My friend! How can you even suggest such a thing? In truth I am shocked!

Most certainly she did not come to me! Ah! She's a wonderful woman, but I am not one of those who is so easily taken in by fine phrases! I am a man of prudence—and I am not the only one! You see, most of those whom she approached responded as I did.

Well-meant though they were, her words were not yet their own. Those whom she approached were mistrustful. But then, they would have mistrusted anyone who had voluntarily chosen the life which had been forced upon them. Just what they held dear, what they had been taught to value—the idea of a life a "little better" than the one they led—she wished to abolish. Why, I would guess that they felt that she was somehow spitting on their dreams.

Thus, more often than not, the advances which she made were repulsed. And yet she stood firm. She had fashioned her vision and was seeking the act. She would never go back to what she had been. It had taken a long while for the first two transitions to occur and she knew that the third would also take some time.

Part Three

I

AH! Listening to her story, I was as attentive and empathetic as always. In fact, her tale produced a profound effect on me. My existence seemed so hollow, so poor . . . After all, she had learned to translate her dream into a demand for action; the dream and the act were unified in her vision and it was clear that she had learned to hope militantly. Nevertheless, I felt better once I realized that there are others whose situations are even more terrible than my own. Some dream without acting, others act without dreaming, and in the lives of such people the dream and the act confront one another as enemies. Cut off from action, the dream bequeaths a harmless optimism; cut off from the dream, the world of action becomes a nightmare. In either case, of course, the militant hope is destroyed.

As for me, well . . . Liquor doesn't help much—but at least it helps a little, eh? Naturally, under normal circumstances I could have done without a drink in the same way as I can do without drugs or women. But, after such a conversation, I felt my situation to be anything but ordinary. Thus, when my gaze fell upon two old acquaintances, you can easily understand what drove me to join them.

Now, that is really unkind, my friend! To accuse me of such a breach of etiquette! No! I most certainly did not go over to them when she was still sitting at my table! After all, what do you take me for?

Besides, the logistics of the situation would have prevented such an advance. You see, for a delicate encounter of this sort, one must always first evaluate the mood of the others. And this, I dare say, can only be accomplished by following a certain set of procedures: a friendly wave of the hand, a knowing nod and—only then—an intimate eye contact. Even after all this, the moments must still be weighed carefully until the most auspicious one arises.

When the moment occurred, my little actress had already gone her way, and so I can tell you that it was with a light step that I made my way to their table and sat down. The two of them sat over there, back against that window which looks so bare without curtains. Though I came to know each of them separately, they had been friends for quite some time—despite the fact that a more unlikely duo would have been hard to imagine.

Even outwardly, they didn't seem to fit together at all. The first sat on his chair like a man of stature, his legs crossed, his stumpy hands, leading into muscular arms, folded in his lap. His hair was brown and dull and, when he wasn't smoking his handmade pipe, he would often mindlessly chew some strands between his thin lips. A set of goldrimmed glasses graced his nose and behind them were eyes which were never still. If it had not been for his stubby teeth he would have been quite attractive, for he radiated health and dressed with style. Thus it was no surprise to see a tailored suit jacket slung over the back of his chair, or a pink and white shirt which beautifully matched his red tie.

As far as his personal characteristics are concerned, well... one could never accuse him of being particularly witty, and yet I really always thought rather well of him—that is until one fine day I asked him to lend me fifty dollars. Clearly a paltry sum if one considers that it would have cemented a friendship! Fifty dollars on a thoroughbred that couldn't lose!

But he refused—and the horse won. Irritating, isn't it?

At any rate, the odds against the success I sought were enormous, for it seemed that this nasty trait of frugality had spread to the other gentlemen in question. In former days, parsimony was not one of his vices, but then the distracted look which he wore was new to him as well. All that remained from the past was the ever-present cigarette dangling from his fingertips which I never once saw him raise to his lips. He was a good deal older than the other fellow. His face was flaccid and pouches hung from his eyes and he was dressed in an old woolen sweater and dungarees.

Oh! It was unnerving that he barely chose to acknowledge my presence. In fact, neither one of them welcomed me in a spirit of true generosity. Nevertheless, I emerged triumphant—even though it was only with an evident show of disdain that they paid for my drink.

And how argumentative they were! Why, as soon as I sat down, the fellow with the pipe asked me—with an unconcealed testiness—what had happened to my monocle. Since there was no purpose to be served in lying, in my normal candid manner I proceeded to tell him that I had decided to give it up and, what's more, that I now heartily regretted what had been nothing more than a foolish affectation. To this, however, the other responded sarcastically: "In other words, you hocked it, didn't you?"

Now, I really should have replied by asking him what had happened to his gun—since I had noticed it at the pawnshop—but then I always make it a practice to ignore remarks as *gauche* as those. Much better than making a fuss, don't you agree my Darling?

So instead of starting trouble I decided to lapse into a wounded silence. Unfortunately, however, this didn't seem to affect them in the least, since they simply returned to the subject they had been discussing before I arrived.

A few sheets of paper lay in front of the one with the glasses, right next to his pipecleaners. As he spoke, he continually toyed with the paper's edges, all the while looking sadly at the floor. It was easy enough to perceive that he was in a state of some agitation.

Why, you ask?

Well, considering the fact that his dear father had left him an estate worth over a quarter of a million dollars on the former's departure from this world, there were only two possibilities.

One: a woman! But then his lover had left him long ago and one would have heard had he seriously taken up with someone else.

Two: his art!

Yes, indeed! I immediately sensed that this was the cause of his despair. You see, in our long and glorious friendship, we had often discussed the most varied aesthetic problems. Oh, how he loved that marvelous quality of creation which defines man's firmest hopes! And then, too, our tastes were so similar! Where others might have thought of Rembrandt or Goethe, we would envision before us a charming pen-and-ink by Beardsley, or a beautifully constructed work by Wilde.

Why?

Well, my reasons remain my own! But he . . . he loved the intricacy, the delicacy of touch, the . . .

Never, how could you even suggest such a thing? Why, my Lady will gladly tell you that the fascination with decadence has nothing at all to do with aesthetic judgment!

Shading, balance, complexity, technique—talent!—was what he loved! Sensitivity, the ability to dream, a touch of mysticism and the languor of melancholy! That was what he admired in masters such as Klimt!

Yes! They are the masters and they deserve appreciation, an appreciation which stems from the deepest roots of sensibility! And my acquaintance felt himself endowed with sensibility! Books, study, rational inquiry, they were nothing but a hindrance, an obstacle to that inspirational quality which he could bring to a work. Inspiration, the blinding light of aesthetic revelation, that was what he believed would lead him down the path of creation: the path which he would follow in order to disclose himself to the world.

Because of his wealth, he could dispose of his time as he wished. Still, although his calling awaited him, there always seemed to be other things which demanded his attention; there was the friend to be comforted, the music to be enjoyed and the marijuana to be smoked—and there was always a ready supply of each!

Look out the window, dearest listener. Do you see that fellow with the sunglasses standing on the corner? He is a recent immigrant, but a man of the streets, nonetheless, and all of us know him well. Hashish, heroin and lovely cocaine—there's nothing which can't be found for the proper price, as my little actress quickly discovered.

But, for the moment, our man of the streets is irrelevant. We were talking about an inspired young fellow and not for one minute did I wish to imply that he neglected his art! No! No! All I wanted to point out was that even artists have other things on their minds!

You see, experience is vital to art. Now, some people have to work. But since my friend didn't have to procure his bread by the sweat of his brow, he sought to find other ways of gaining experience.

Still, the activity taking place in the great world around him seemed to mean so little! It was so much easier, so much more meaningful, so much more artistic, to give way to fantasy! Politics? The social world? What, does it all matter? Particularly if it continually gets in the way of the expression of a man's soul? The outer world is only ephemeral anyway—it is the *essence* of man which endures—and so the external world meant nothing to this writer who wished to define the essence of the human condition through fiction.

Unfortunately, his stories were never published. Still, he kept trying. Having too much pride for a vanity publisher, he spent a good part of his time running from one agent to another with the drafts in order to explain the future importance of his work and the obvious necessity for its publication. Thus, it was easy for me to conclude that yet another rejection had come to pass during the day in question. Consequently, at the first opportune moment—though with my usual tact!—I resolved to ask whether this was indeed the case.

Oh! It's impossible to imagine the animosity which my cordial inquiry provoked! Why, the fellow turned positively livid! He hurled abuses at me and, had his companion not caught his arm, I'm sure that he would have dealt me quite a blow. In fact, the maniac had already risen from his chair and was brandishing his fist in my face. Still, in spite of his neanderthal-like behavior, I remained perfectly composed. I can even tell you that his anguish touched my soul.

Of course, it took some time before he calmed down. Afterwards, however, he looked so meek, so timid . . . Thus, after I emerged from under the table, I suggested, in a conciliatory tone, that he read us some selections from what he had lying in front of him on the table.

But do you know what he did instead?

He took all three drinks—mine was almost empty, thank God!—and poured them over the small stack of papers in front of him. Then he grabbed his manuscript, rushed over to the garbage, and stuffed his soggy masterpiece into the can. Exhausted, he returned to us and sank down into his chair. Of course, within minutes, he felt dreadfully ashamed. In fact, he begged us to forgive him and offered to refill our glasses—an offer to which I only grudgingly agreed, since I abhor outbursts of that sort.

Yet, his embarrassment was sincere. Why, he even ran over to the waitress to hurry our order along, before proceeding to retrieve his work. Ruefully, he sat down once again and then, in the most natural motion which one could possibly imagine, placed both hands over his face and slowly began to rub his eyes.

Inwardly tortured, he mused aloud whether now even his dreams had become worthless—at which point, both the other fellow and myself began to contradict him in unison.

Yes, for him, truly there was only the dream. The world of action was such a bore, reality was so meaningless, and besides he found it impossible to communicate—let alone to act. Somehow, his thoughts always found themselves transvalued whenever he put them into words. The first would only contradict the second, and the second the third, until knots formed within the sentences and the paragraphs. They all became twisted and these twisted words spilled over from the page into his life. Reality became a shambles which he could neither conceptualize nor express, a jumble in which there were neither questions nor answers. Words seemed to leap from his touch until, finally, everything which he said or thought came to be drawn into reality's circle of chaos.

Only the dream existed as an alternative. Yet, precisely because he flew to the dream with such unthinking haste, his fantasies became false; they became tinged with his own anxieties and the repressions of a world which he did not care to understand. Thus, his fantasy never quite unlocked the kingdom of the new; his fantasies were never quite radical enough, for he never even contemplated how they might enter the world. And so the dream became sacrosanct and his hopes were left hanging, while his soul—and the existant as well—appeared to him as a hell in ruins.

Nevertheless, he clung to his tattered fantasies and treasured them. Thus, I wasn't in the least surprised when, on that particular evening, this fellow exclaimed that he would read us nothing, but instead would tell us of an extraordinary dream.

It seems that this dream occurred to him during an afternoon on which he had come down with a headache. Lying on his bed, he fell into a half-sleep, an easy prey for my Lady whose spells are cast best in the bleak twilight of a muggy day. Tossing and turning, it was surely my Lady's heaven that he saw since, for once, his descriptions were fluid and his language cogent.

I raise my glass to you, my Love! To your conquest! And it all began with a man sitting in a cage smack in the middle of a jungle—a jungle in its foliage, glistening and alive with the exotic colors and sensations of that which has never been. The Man looked out from between the bars while behind him two others appeared in the cage.

Probably an aristocrat of old, the one was scrupulously clean, exquisitely tailored and marked with the finest facial contours. The light from what seemed to be an emerald gleaming in the sun—though this was a world without sun—bronzed the beginnings of a blond beard and accentuated the crisp blue eyes. Immediately, he started sizing up the second fellow who screamed endlessly as his fists reverberated on the bars. No doubt a parvenu, the second was gaudily dressed and a watch without hands hung from his flabby wrist. There was not a hair on his head, and his neck was almost obscured by layers of fat.

The antipathy between the two was instinctual. The aristocrat taunted his companion who, in turn, battered him to the floor. Again and again, the aristocrat would rise, begin his bickering and find himself on his back. The ritual went on until, suddenly, an axe appeared in the sky. But it vanished instantly as the bars of the cage flew open and the two men disappeared from sight.

It was then that the first Man found himself thrown out into that grievous paradise—thrown out alone, without a friend, into what had become a wasteland with only that emerald-like entity to relieve the boredom of his vision. Lazily he reached for it, only to watch it jump from his hand. Then he leaped at it, but to no avail. The emerald, that magical *fata morgana*, moved horizontally forward, at a level just above his head, and the Man began to chase after it.

The dreamer said that he felt his mouth open in his sleep. Space was one color and yet, with each physical movement of the Man, the color changed—from red to green to purple to orange to yellow until, finally, the single colors turned into a *mélange.* The Man travelled far; hills, swamps, forests, and prairies rose up behind him. Out of breath, he stopped, and a lake of rubies appeared at his feet. The lake sparkled brilliantly, so brilliantly that its force momentarily blinded him.

It was then that the emerald overhead began its transformation. Athena's hand touched his face while Aphrodite whispered an immoral proposition in his ear; Zeus threw his thunderbolts while the Furies pinpricked his body. From the corner of his eye he saw Dionysus vomit while Apollo stood laughing on the side. Bricks of gold glimmered before the wanderer's eyes as fame, immortality, ecstasy and wonder assumed carnate form. The change was continuous; yet, after each and just before the next, the mass always reverted for an instant to its emerald-like shape.

And for the Man, it all took so much time in a world without time. His beard turned stringy and tufts of hair started to fall from his head. He became old overnight. His teeth began to rot, and still onward he walked—or crawled. Above him the emerald glittered as gangs beat him with chains and forced him to drink their urine in the moment before they disappeared. Afterwards, for a time, he would lie in the dust with his lips puffed and one eye swollen shut. Crusts of blood were layered on his face and the pus began to form where his fingernails once had been.

Never enough! No rest for the weary! Once again he would slowly rise to his feet and then, once more, begin to chase what hovered beyond him. Often in the emerald's light, faces would appear: animals' faces drenched in acid, the faces of lepers and mutilated children, faces worn down by years of apathy, absurd clowns' masks, expressionless faces, and then the face of death itself in all its purity—always the same faces rotating in the same order. Faster and faster they rotated until the Man could stand no more. He fell to his knees with his fists pressed against his eyes. Pain emerged before him, dimensionally, as a thing—as a crustacean into whose pincers he found himself drawn. Terror seized him and, from the blackness, disconnected eyes spewed out a judgment.

At that moment, he almost found himself to be free. His world became placid; the sound of water running over rocks came to his ears and he felt the warm grass beneath his feet. Trees sprouted from the ground and gentle furry animals nuzzled at his body. The emerald moved towards him and he reached for it. It entered his grasp lovingly and turned into a flower—a blue flower which seemed so very delicate and so very strong. But it instantly turned back into an emerald once again, a translucent emerald. His hand passed through it and an electric joy seized him. It was then that he started to sink into what must have been quicksand.

The other men returned. At first they tried to help him, but they didn't know what to do; their noses dissolved and each blamed the other. Meanwhile, mud flooded the Man's mouth and strangled his cries. When he regained consciousness, he was back with the other two in the same cage which they had formerly occupied, only now it was enveloped in a radiant silver light.

Later the sky turned violet; how it was impossible to say. Still, there was no sun. The emerald was gone and a gentleman in uniform came to open the door of the cell. Only two men were found alive, however, and their hands were trembling. The third lay with one eye open staring at a cockroach on the ceiling of what had become a room. A river of blood flowed from the wound in his head. Unnaturally distended, his tongue reached down to his shoulders and there were marks around his throat. The axe lay in a corner, ignored like a dirty rag, but that blue flower had forced its way through the cement floor and was glimmering brightly.

As a guard led the two men outside, neither could look at the corpse. They walked next to each other; neither was thinking of the flower, one man was looking at his hands while the other was desperately trying to wipe the sticky blood from his coat...

Well, now you have heard the dream of that sensitive and wealthy man. You see, even the wealthy have their fears and hopes. Thus it wasn't surprising that, once the last word of the dream had fallen from his lips, the dreamer's demeanor took on the fragrant air of expectation. It was easy enough to surmise that this dream was, in fact, no dream at all; that instead, it was something which had been planned, created and perfected—only to what purpose I can't precisely say.

But, no matter! He had achieved one goal at last. There's no denying it, his artistic sensibility finally burst into the open—only neither of us who sat with him knew exactly how to respond. Thus, I discreetly pulled out my handkerchief to blow my nose, while the other half of the audience shifted his cigarette nervously from one hand to the other.

Ah, my Lady! It was a forceful silence which engulfed us! So, after returning the handkerchief to my pocket, I found myself obliged to comment on what had transpired. With what must have been a real fervor in my voice, I remarked upon the magnificence of the dream's imagery—even though that image of the blue flower sounded rather familiar. Then I proceeded to explain that the story's humanistic implications could not be denied. Indeed, I wished to go on to say that such wonderful optimism in the face of horror was praiseworthy to say the least, and that I had been captivated from the narrative's beginning to its close.

Only suddenly I found myself interrupted in mid-sentence.

Now I was never one to quibble over a point of order! No, I didn't even try to contend with that chainsmoker's rudeness. Besides, I could sense that a terrible argument was about to begin.

Still, the listener sounded so very sad as he gave his response to the story, and I knew that it hurt him to maintain that this symbolic flower meant nothing; that it was foolish to even consider such symbols since the horror of reality could never be abolished.

The dreamer turned very pale, but the listener would not retreat from his position. The listener shook his head while he argued that the dreamer's conception of existence was based on nothing other than a useless romantic belief in hope.

I remember how the dreamer's hands began to tremble as his eyes searched out this friend whom he thought he knew so well. Finally, he lashed out at the listener:

"Pessimism! As if that's the answer! A pessimism without hope or beauty! I know, you'll tell me about the Greeks and their pessimism. But they believed in fate and arbitrary gods. Yet there is no fate, there are no gods, and in fact, it's from the Greeks that we can see that men are better than the gods they construct. The Greek hero disobeyed the gods—but to you that means nothing. A hopeless gesture! But I say that the action itself implies hope!"

The listener's thoughts were vague and uneven. Yet, he made it clear that at least there was action—that it was the action which justified the hero and not any abstract symbolic hope. And, as he went on, he claimed that it was too easy to live in ecstatic blindness like the seers; that the true rebel, the real man of daring, is the one who does not accept the warmth of the sun or the softness of a flower.

The argument continued until both fell silent. Then, however, a frightful anger entered the listener's voice as he shouted from the void that there is nothing grand about anguish or suffering. For him, there was nothing to be praised in the story of the Man—that misery is ugly, that it is simply a lack, an emptiness which can never be filled. "What results from your story is a type of thinking which ignores reality and the choices one must make, all in the name of a beautiful fantasy—and that's not enough for me."

The dreamer didn't quite know how to respond at first. He began one thought, only to drop it a moment later to try another. No! This dreamer just couldn't understand the listener's disgust. But I knew better. I knew that the dreamer's story had struck at the listener's heart.

And, as I looked at this listener, I could see him formulating his words. Never had I seen him deliberate so! I saw him looking back across time, glancing at me and seeing in me a partial reflection of himself, ages upon ages ago.

The listener's cigarette had burned down to the filter and I felt a pungent odor fill my nostrils. The words came to him naturally. It even startled me when I realized how very soft his voice had grown as he expressively described an elderly housewife whom he had met on his second trip abroad while passing through a village in the land where the fiercest tyranny had reigned.

Apparently, while he was at her house for dinner, she began to tell him of her brother who was once a member of that brown-shirted group of thugs who policed the country. But she spoke of him tenderly and explained that her brother had been good to his wife and children, and that she and he had always been very close—even though (and she made this clear) she had staunchly opposed his politics from the very first.

On the mantle, next to the dining room table, there was a picture of him. No doubt it was easy to imagine—just from the fellow's bearing in the photograph—how proud he must have been to wear his brown shirt and how his polished black boots must have glistened in the sun.

The listener became more and more intense as he continued. On a given night, late at night—they always went on their calls late at night—this young man was ordered to arrest a certain family, just as he had been ordered before on numerous occasions. Two colleagues were with him as this woman's brother approached the house. One of them remained on the street as the other followed the protagonist up the three flights of stairs.

While the other soldier guarded the hall, this lady's brother smashed his riflebutt through the door. It was a one room apartment in which an old woman, a child and the child's mother lived. The infant started to scream at the noise and, when the man finally broke through, the mother scooped the infant up in her arms, fell to her knees and began to beg this man with the all-too-familiar uniform not to shoot.

Now, strange as it may sound, it seems that the soldier hesitated. The housewife told the listener that her brother explained to her afterwards that he had never before seen such a beautiful foreign face. Her face was of an oval shape and her green eyes—which glowed so brightly with fear—touched him to the point where he could shout no commands; embracing the trigger of his gun, his finger felt paralyzed.

The housewife went on to say that her brother had never disobeyed an order before. Still, he turned his back and walked out the door. In the hall he told his waiting comrade that he could neither kill the little group nor take them away to be killed.

The fellow's colleague understood, squeezed the young man's shoulder gently, and promised that he wouldn't be reported. Then the fellow went inside. The housewife maintained that her brother swore to her that tears rolled down his eyes when he heard the flurry of machine gun bullets: there was nothing he could have done to help them.

The forms were filled out later—the family had been shot while resisting arrest. After that, the man went back to his duties; the young man's friend was true to his word and the moment of hesitation was never reported. This, however, proved to be immaterial. Indeed, the housewife nearly broke down as she told of how both men were killed during the purge in which it was decided that the country's dominant color would be changed from brown to black.

A human tragedy! What do you say to that, my friend?!

For his part, the dreamer said nothing—that is until all the blood had finally run from his face. Then, however, he let forth a stream of verbiage. He demanded to know what this story had to do with his dream. He maintained over and over again that the listener had understood nothing; that because the listener had refused to acknowledge the liberating power of the dream, he had to shatter it by comparing the dream to the most terrible aspects of reality. And then the dreamer finally said that the dream must stand alone, that it dare not be constrained by any of the consequences which someone may wish to draw from it. The dream, he said, is a rarefied form of license and . . .

The dreamer kept talking, but the listener didn't reply. Yet it was clear that an unhappiness was chilling his soul as he rose from the table and slowly began to move toward the door. The dreamer grabbed his beautiful jacket and, catching up with his companion, followed him into the street. The dreamer continued to protest and, in an imploring tone, tried to make himself understood. Once again foresaken, from my chair, I heard their words fade into the night.

II

So many visions in so few words! Cluttered perceptions interspersed among each other! New dreams are born, old ones pass away as stories—but action remains!

Yes! A world of activity always remains! But without its dreams, this world is flat, empty; as it lacks the hope of a better tomorrow, everything is permitted today. Indeed, look around and you'll see that a vapid nihilism rules! My Lady knows that this is a world in which a man looks at his neighbor and finds only another restless self, searching for a meaning which he can never embrace by feverishly jumping from one activity to another, until finally . . .

So take care in judging this dreamer of ours! Perhaps he did play the fool by divorcing his hopes from the activity of the world, but perhaps he also sensed the danger of activity divorced from the dream. Through the dream he could at least believe that the present could be transcended, but in a world without dreams even the desire for transcendence is either lost or perverted.

It's true! So many dreams are spun, so many stories are told, and without the social world it is impossible to decide upon the validity of the hopes which a dream contains. Just look at the dreamer and it's easy to see that, without the possibility of such a decision, the sphere of fantasy is anarchic. Yes, it is a frightful chaos in which there is no one to trust; thus, one remains isolated within the space of one's own desires.

Miserable wretch that he was! The dreamer could only believe that his dreams belonged to him alone—that they were what differentiated him from others, that they were all that he could preserve from a reality which was deflating everything around him. And . . . Oh! How terrible it is to dream alone!

But, lucky soul that you are, before you sits a man who realizes the need to share one's dreams—and this is the need I seek to awaken in you!

With that in mind, you shouldn't be too quick in judging our listener either. For, no matter how sober his responses may have sounded, beneath it all were his own visions, visions from which he wished to escape. For you see, he was a man with no responsibilities, a man who had rejected the heavens so that he might secure himself to the earth—and now he no longer found himself able to raise his head. For him there was only the act; there was no place for the dream—and so, finally, hope died in his heart.

Oh! I remember how we met! I remember how I felt that it was time for a change and how I decided to leave my dear café to board a plane which would soar through the sky like a thunderbolt. I'll never forget my exhilaration as I disembarked! There I stood in the capital of chance, in the lazy heat of the afternoon, with thoughts of the night to come. Forty-eight hours later—just a touch the worse for wear—I found myself at the party where the two of us first met.

The moment I arrived, I gravitated towards him. You see, in those days he still possessed a vibrant strength of character which can always be detected—particularly in surroundings as strange as those of an engagement party held on the outskirts of a city of sin.

I had met the happy bride on the night before. In a quiet little lounge, removed from the ghastly clatter of slot machines, she had asked me over to her table to share a bottle of wine. Alas! Truth to tell, I was in a vile mood—for reasons which can be easily deduced. I found myself disliking her from the very first—for she had the terrible habit of making light of the misfortunes of another. But, always the gentleman, I was as cordial as could be.

"Friendliness is its own reward!" I thought, as we prepared to leave together. As luck would have it, in the morning I received my due: an invitation to the little gathering which was planned for the following evening.

Though I was busy, I couldn't refuse a request to be present at the most important moment of her life. Yet, when I arrived at the party, my mouth dropped. People spoke in muted tones, and with the exception of the gentleman with the broad-brimmed hat, the small company was neatly paired off. Also, I must say—*en passant* of course!—that unfortunately, in contrast to what I had been led to believe, the food proved to be of poor quality.

The gentleman wearing the broad-brimmed hat sat alone, his hands folded in his lap, with a cigarette sticking upright between his fingers. Sitting across from him in a soft leather armchair, I noticed that his head was bent backwards and that his half-closed eyes were looking up at the ceiling.

Thinking that there might be something up there which would give me food for thought, I looked up too. I saw nothing save the cracks which ran across the ceiling like the arteries of a woman's leg. But then they seemed to unite as the white ceiling turned murky grey; it spread its jaws and yawned, enveloping me so that I felt myself cast adrift within it. Images of the grave leapt to mind, acrid odors of the casket! Dreadful sensations from which I felt the need to escape at any cost.

Conversation became imperative and so I broke the ice with that stranger by courteously remarking on the beauty of his hat. In response, however, he only lowered his head, curled his lips into a sullen grin, and sluggishly told me that one day he just might make me a present of it.

Even were I in a better mood, I would have been shocked by

the impudence of such an offer! But, then, I felt that need for conversation and so replied: "How nice."

At this he laughed heartily and, after broadly waving towards a group of ladies (which included his bride-to-be), made a pronouncement. Indeed, with the sweeping gesture of a monarch, he exclaimed that he had slept with all of them—and that they were all so miserable in bed that he was wondering whether they had ever taken lessons from each other. Everyone was horrified and so, probably for good measure, he threw in that he was blindly drunk.

Now, though the truth of his first claim was questionable, that of the second was decidedly not. He was drunk; indeed he was so drunk that he could barely articulate his words.

I can only tell you that the bride-to-be was beside herself. Her face was crimson as she rushed over to him, yelling that she had had enough and that the marriage was off, whereupon she ran into the bedroom in order to have a good cry.

Slumped in his chair, my companion was the picture of passivity. Still, I could sense that he had taken a liking to me. So, after begging the good ladies' pardon for his rudeness, I invited myself to join him for a drink from the bottle which had been resting between his thighs.

Spilling more than a drop over the brim of my glass, he somehow managed to make clear that it had taken a conscientious effort for him to attain the level of intoxication at which I was then privileged to see him. He had apparently begun his self-assigned task at precisely ten o'clock that morning and had continued steadily on his course until he had finally reached his fiancée's door. Though it was a miracle that he had even found the address, I couldn't help asking whether he had remembered to bring her a present. In response, he proudly pointed—though with a shaky hand—to a rather large pineapple which was now sitting in the middle of the living room table. He had picked it up from some fruitstand along the way. Though his bride was appalled at his condition, she was nevertheless delighted at the gift; thus the pineapple had brought about a temporary peace.

Ah, my dearest friend! What a lovely conversation we were

having when, suddenly, wagging his index finger, he motioned me to come closer. Almost in a whisper, he gravely asked me whether I could possibly understand what it was like to be condemned to feel oneself a man *only occasionally.*

After fanning away the whiff of alcohol, I thought for a moment and then said that I knew very well. It was with these words that, after almost tumbling over the coffee table which separated us, he threw his arm around my shoulder. His cries rang in my ears over and over again: "Oh, you do understand! Finally, I've found you!"

I confess, of course, that I was somewhat taken aback. Ever wary of making a scene—particularly since my hostess had returned, rather puffy-eyed, from the bedroom—I thought it might be best to continue our discussion in less emotionally charged surroundings. But, while I was virtually pushing him out the door, he kept looking back as he imploringly whispered in my ear: "Occasionally, only occasionally! Isn't it horrible?!"

I made no reply. For you can be sure that I had my hands full, with him in one arm and the half-empty bottle of scotch tucked under the other. But he didn't give up. After letting him sink onto the stoop of a house across the street in order to catch my breath, he looked up at me and undoubtedly decided that a different approach was necessary if he was to gain my attention.

How well I remember his lecherous look of comradeship as he inquired of me why I thought he should have gone to the trouble of seducing all those women. I had an answer ready. But, before I could get a word in, he gave me his reason: the mania which overcame him, which scorched his temples during that string of nights when even the walls seemed to torment him with thoughts of nothingness.

Even then, he never dreamed. Alone in his room, he would cup his hands and find them empty. That was all he could understand, and his life . . . In the quiet hours of the morning he would search for memories, though there were never any within reach. There was only the present, an unchanging rotation of days in which each seemed to be brought into the ever-widening circle which encompassed those that had come before. Memory languished in the chasm between truth and wish—and he experienced anguish. But it was a subtle anguish, neither burning nor intense —more like the dull throbbing of a low fever.

"Were it only so," he thought. "Could it not have been otherwise?" he questioned. Suspended in the chasm, the past became free—far more so than what he then saw as his future. Open and pliable, he felt the past present itself in such a way as to be immediately resurrected into a structured future—which somehow always seemed to be falling backwards.

But, of course, the days pushed ahead, carrying him and his mania along with him. What he needed was company in despair, company in facing an illusionary future. Thus he began to look for someone, anyone, it didn't matter who—so long as they could lie together, so long as he could smell her body and feel her hair upon his chest.

He chose partner after partner. They came and went. With each he felt the lack of that sense of duration for which he longed; to each the same story with the missing words had to be told until, finally, he settled on a partner—a partner for the duration. With her, he thought, he could share a memory. But immediately the question arose: a memory of what? This, he found himself free to choose—but only within the circle of the past. Undetermined by what he was, he nevertheless felt himself chained to what he would become.

There was nothing for which to hope. Only liquor and work existed. Through the first he could see freedom's paradox, the paradox of future and past; through the second . . . Well, one fine day it occurred to him that all the while he was thinking about the idea of freedom, he was engaged in selling the only practical freedom that he owned: the labor which supported his life.

Just think my friend! Exchanging a stretch of one's life for a paycheck! This must have been the thought which ravaged his brain while he was lying on his back, beneath a car, adjusting the axle. Looking up, it was as if he were peering into the auto's open belly. Everything seemed so senseless, so wasted. He saw himself pouring his life into a disposable routine—until the moment when he would be no more. What then? No one would remember him and within a week no one would care whether he had ever walked the earth or not.

There was no one to whom he could express himself. He could not speak to his co-workers; such topics were banned by tacit consent. He could not go to his union; its leaders were as anonymous as those who controlled the corporation which owned the garage.

But then, suddenly, he felt a drop of oil slowly sliding down his arm and little by little, yet with the persistence of a thick fluid's movement, the existence which he had always led began to disintegrate. He began to laugh more and, sometimes, he would even believe that the moment had caught fire. On such nights he fell happily asleep with his partner for the duration, thinking that his freedom had finally taken on some semblance of content—which it did, after a fashion.

Yet, he told me, when he awoke on the morning of his engagement, he finally understood that freedom was too cramped when confined to the space between the blanket and the sheet. Putting on his underwear, incomplete memories of tomorrow once again offered their temptation—and the chasm grew wider.

"Only occasionally," he had said. But occasionally wouldn't suffice. Especially after work, he would always feel restless and need to feel himself doing something, anything, so long as it didn't involve selling more of his blood to the indistinguishable shadows. Nothing he did, however, gave him any satisfaction. First, he tried to write, and then to paint, but he showed no talent for either. Too honest to believe that he could create for himself alone, he ended up pursuing neither the color nor the word.

She, who was to be his bride, had a healthy income; he had none. Before he met her, he had taken what money he had saved out of the bank, bought himself the dashing headpiece which I so admired, and decided to travel.

What else was there for him to do? Believing that society had ostracized him, he gently pushed ever further into his own stifling loneliness while ostensibly traversing continents. Yes, it was with sore feet and a fatigued spirit that he trekked inward and felt the world constraining him—a world which would never change. But then a gushing, surging emotion arose in his soul—an emotion which carried away all that stood in its path! No wonder that, ultimately, whatever connection remained to them, the others should have been irretrievably lost.

Twice denied! Just as he was unable to find solace in the musty museums that housed works which he had never been taught to understand, he was equally unable to find hope in the faces of those whom he felt that he could never know. Society receded from his vision; each person, in any country and on any sidewalk, became only another facet of an existence which he would never be able to savor properly; each landscape became nothing more than a fleeting glimpse of beauty that too would pass.

He came to stand before himself ever more directly—to the exclusion of all else. The world with its richness and diversity came to be drained of its dynamism and thus, without hurry or resolution, while roaming the world without purpose, he gradually began to dismiss his life.

Ha! Ha! How silly you look! I can tell from your expression, my friend, that until this very moment you were one of those who believed that such a dismissal involves either a grand gesture or a grander cause!

Nonsense! In this world of mine, one is never able to pinpoint a cause, and the result is that one piddles away one's life a droplet at a time, until the droplets form a stream which flows outward to the sea, always to the sea . . . And this fellow was no different from the rest. All that his dismissal entailed was a perspectiveless perseverance which led him . . .

Isolated in his activity, our wanderer's actions turned stale and the world reeked of death. In fact, death became a taste in his mouth, the last and most pitifully inadequate assurance of his singularity. Unique, enclosed within his self-woven cocoon, he could only peek out at his actions as if they had been performed by someone else. Thus he gained a perverse innocence. Beyond men, suspended above the actions of others, his unique freedom became an unbearable horror.

I think of it all now. The specks of the future were there

in the present, but neither one of us had the insight. Oh! If only we had the insight! Or the foresight! Or . . .

Bah! What does it matter! My Angel knows that there is not much room for conjecture when one is faced with a drunkard's frenzy. I tried to calm him, but somehow he knew that I was taking in his words. So it shouldn't come as any surprise that by the time I had half-carried him, half-dragged him to his room, our friendship had been sealed. Then, too, it isn't difficult to understand that, after sprawling him out on a chair, I felt there would be little harm in my using his bed.

And I was right, too! For, on the following morning, after a rather groggy awakening, he proceeded to thank me profusely for all my help. Indeed, with the break of dawn, a period of time began during which we were inseparable.

How marvelous those days were! We went everywhere together. There was still money in his pocket and he spent it with an abandon which pleased my soul. True, he was often moody. Still, he laughed gaily at the theater and took part with great verve in the activities offered in those lascivious houses of ill repute. Those were our diversions and, when they proved dull, there was always the casino.

Yes, my Lady! The casino! Most delightfully garish—and most hospitable—of worlds! Each one is open twenty-four hours a day for the owners know that greed never subscribes to regular hours.

There were bright dazzling lights and entertainment as well! In one casino, trapeze artists floated gracefully above the noisy crowd and, in another, the finest classical music complemented the steady spinning of the roulette wheel. In a third, there were cowboys with imitation spurs, while a fourth offered the most delectable young ladies dressed up as pussycats, whose aesthetic presence would not fail to offset any material loss.

How discordant it all seemed! And yet, as with a twelve tone symphony, there was a unity which bound these disparate clashing phenomena into an interlocking whole. But no matter how overwhelming the total effect, there was always a particular privacy granted to the participants who sought their singular confrontation with fate. Each was separated from his neighbor, closed off to the latter's existence. There wasn't even any human competition between players—to the one, the other was simply nonexistent. Even at the poker tables, adversaries were faceless beings who were passed over as quickly as if they were files in a bureau drawer. They were there to be looked at, sized up, beaten, and forgotten.

But, of course, there are some individuals who are not quite so easy to forget. Can you imagine that one morning we were privileged to see a fellow with a week's growth of beard, a tramp's clothes, and the most emaciated hands, win at baccarat to the tune of approximately fourteen thousand dollars?

He won consistently for almost an hour. But then, when he lost a paltry hand for two hundred dollars, what do you think he did? Well, right there in front of everyone, he burst into tears, lit a matchbook to his money, pulled a gun from his pocket and, with a quick squeeze of the trigger, blew his brains out.

Bang! Just like that! All in the space of thirty seconds.

What a mess he made! Everyone was cleared away almost instantly. Yet, while the tidying-up procedure was taking place, my once-again intoxicated companion nimbly managed to pick up the dead man's revolver. The others didn't notice; the background of tieless shirts, bermuda shorts, and diamond rings simply mulled around while low voices commented on the tragedy. Within minutes, however, everyone was back at his slot machine—although one or two people did see the suicide as an omen and left for another casino.

Only the cripples did not let themselves be interrupted. Not one of them batted an eyelash. And there were so many of them! Wheelchairs blocked the aisles and crutches were to be seen surrounding the dice tables. All of them seemed to play dice. Each one was ready at any moment to receive Fortuna's recompense for the blows which an unjust destiny had delivered upon him. Every one of them believed that his infirmity entitled him to a reward and so each roll of the dice became a demand for retribution, as if the seat of judgment had been shifted to that green felt table upon which those ivory cubes were being tossed.

Absurd! As if Fortuna ever kept accounts!

Why just consider that poor suicide! My companion understood perfectly that had the tramp won half that amount or double that amount, it still would have happened in exactly the same way.

You see, at the tables, what drives such a soul is not money but power! Oh! I can still see how he sought to clasp those moments of power to his chest! But the triumph of power is fragile in an isolated universe for there is never a standard by which it can be measured. One looks to the unconquerable absolute and finds that suddenly the moment of risk has surpassed the quest for power! In this way, power undermines itself. All that remains is the uncertainty of triumph, the questionable force of one's own will.

This self-denying risk, carried out in the name of one's personal will, was what led this tramp to his downfall. But then, standing next to the black-jack table, I suddenly realized that my companion was just like him. Sheepishly, this listener looked at me while, with his hand in his pocket, he gingerly fingered his ill-gotten gain. He informed me that he only had about eight dollars left. Giving me the change, he laid the eight bills on the table.

The dealer dealt the cards, one face down and one showing: a six to my benefactor and an eight to himself. Bending the bottom card up for me to see, my companion and I stared at a king. Sixteen! I would have stood firm. But my friend knocked the table and received a seven. He was over twenty-one; he had lost. The dealer took in the money and the cards. We never did see what he had.

Silently, we walked out to a large fountain which stood in front of the casino. Two children were playing in the water, I didn't leave him—there was no need. I simply asked if I could watch and he somberly nodded his head in agreement.

And why shouldn't he have agreed? Why does someone on a ledge wait for a crowd to assemble before he jumps?

Because, dearest listener, he will want those last seconds to be made precious. Even if, up to that very point, this individual has considered his life to be nothing more than a meager fabrication, he will want those last moments to be engraved in eternity—and so he needs his witness, his accomplice.

Go on! Laugh, my vicious Darling! Still, I tell you that those last seconds must count! For such a decision to be made, one must believe that they will count like no others before them!

Naturally, however, I sensed a barrier being erected between us. I can't say for certain what he was thinking, but his head was bent as he walked and it wouldn't have surprised me in the least if he were in fact counting the cracks in the cement.

He absent-mindedly stopped a few yards from the fountain. The night was innocuous; a few stars seemed to float mechanically through the sky, tugged along by clouds which formed no pattern whatsoever. The spray from the large white fountain caused his face to glisten in its light. Turning away from me, he watched the spurts of water shoot through the air. Then he took off his hat and handed it to me. As I was brushing it off, I saw his gaze focus on the children.

The smaller one was about seven, and she splashed about with that shrill delight which so often grates upon one's nerves. The other, probably her sister, was somewhat older. She was perhaps twelve or thirteen; her blond hair was straight and thick, and her face already held that look of sultry sexuality which marks a desirable woman. When she smiled, her tongue flickered out to moisten her lips. She was just entering puberty and I can still see before me the beginnings of what would soon become heavenly breasts breaking through her blouse. Her body was well tanned and her hard muscles made her flesh smooth.

My companion looked at her intently while slowly pulling the gun from his pocket. He lifted it with a wooden arm but, instead of bringing the revolver up to his temple, he pointed the muzzle at her. And then . . .

Well, then, my friend, I saw his face become grotesque with the look of evil. The planes of his head became distorted and his mouth began to droop at one end. He turned completely white and perspiration appeared on his forehead, the droplets running like rain down his nose.

Suddenly, however, his features became concentrated into a frightening stare, and, as he lowered the pistol to his side, his tongue flew out, sweeping out over his lips in near mimickry of the child. He grabbed his hat abruptly and, without another word, began to walk away.

But then, on what must have been second thought, he stepped back a few paces and handed the hat back to me. With an angry snarl, a hiss of power, I heard him say: "Now I can act! There is nothing which binds me! I owe nothing to anyone, and now I can be free. There's nothing left but license!" Then he strolled over to the child and began speaking to her. I saw him gently stroke her face and her arms. Within minutes, they were walking off together, his hand on her shoulder, his mouth close to her neck.

Now, I have always been a man of tolerance and discretion. Consequently, it didn't even cross my mind to follow them. I never saw the child again and, when I finally ran into my former companion, it was many years later.

He had taken his second trip to Europe and had changed visibly. He was thinner, almost gaunt, and his brow was deeply furrowed; his skin had taken on a sickly yellowish tinge and he no longer wore a hat over what had become a balding skull.

I learned that he was working at the check-out counter of a supermarket and that he had taught himself to play the piano. Unfortunately, however, I also found out that we had very little left in common. Thus, I saw him only rarely after that. In fact, I immediately sensed that—for some reason or another—he had taken a dislike to me. Naturally, neither of us ever mentioned the thoughts which had ravaged his past; the future alone was what existed now.

Part Four

I

I fear that all this has served to put a damper on the evening! Your expression is so very sober! How depressing our café has become! I confess that it was thoughtless of me to have gone on so. No! You're quite right, my Love! Something must be done! Of course, it's difficult to change one's mood at the drop of a hat, but still one must do what one can. Besides, in a place like this, one must learn how to transform one's attitude. Here, you see, a man must live like a chameleon since—if one only takes the trouble to look around—it is easy to see what happens when existence becomes trapped within a single frame of mind.

So let us move away from the grand issues and the half-baked concerns to the concrete and the simple. For there are those who ask only for a little security in an untenable world of license, and who hope that the fury of the dream can be tamed. Wearied by the world, confused by ideas, these people long for escape.

Take that fellow standing outside. Can you see him there, through the window—the one with dark glasses and the brown leather coat? I met him on a trip to a city which lies across the ocean: a city of spires and culture, of delicacy and grace. It was there that he embarked on his attempt to obtain a bit of contentment and security. Such simple desires . . .

Part ruffian, part thief, part drug pusher and confidence man, I found him calculating and cynical from the first. He was a man of the streets, however—and so, a man after my own heart.

Don't be fooled, there was nothing romantic or adventurous about his life! My Lady will tell you that it's no easy task squeezing twenty dollars out of a junkie, or collecting an overdue gambling debt from a man with a mistress to support. Who knows what a given wristwatch is really worth, or even the price of a night's pleasure? Furthermore, there are the various ailments one catches standing on street corners, the harassment from the authorities—and nowhere the least sign of affection. Is it any wonder then that he wished to get away from the streets?

I remember: we were together in a place much like this one when he told me that he was fed up—that, finally, thoughts of happiness, comfort and companionship, were calling to him like the half-forgotten words of a melody sung by an old *chanteuse.* I remember: I looked around with his eyes—and everything seemed so stale! I remember: the sawdust on the floor, the thick smoke which poisoned the air, the dirty ashtray between us, and that relentless, listless, blaring music.

This was the atmosphere which molded his thoughts on the night he made his decision to marry. He had not yet chosen his bride of course. But he had a plan. He dragged me over to his little room and immediately went for the telephone book. With a flick of the wrist, meaningless names appeared before his eyes!

Anonymity revealed! A random page, the number next to an average female's name and *presto!* Clammy fingers were tightening around the phone. He dialed carefully and after a few seconds of silence I heard the sound of his steady voice. Within moments, it was agreed that he should meet this faceless woman on the following evening.

What's that? Impossible, you say?

So, you challenge the truth that is to be found in fiction? You, who have already been witness to my own powers of persuasion! You, who have seen why I never lose an argument!

Before meeting me, would you have considered me *possible?* Improbable, at the most—but here I am, in the flesh and breathing! Why then should you deny the possibilities of characters whom you don't even know? What if I were to tell you that the woman was impressed with the fellow's candor, what if she liked the tone of his voice? What if she were taken with thoughts of adventure? I'm shocked at your lack of imagination, and I dare say that . . .

Oh, but please! You needn't get up! Don't even bother to apologize! You see, I wasn't really offended and, on thinking it over, I will admit that all this does sound a bit unlikely. Yet, most intimate companion, what is rare, what is truly occasional, always appears first as improbable. Still, you know yourself that the improbable occurs—that it is precisely this which separates it from the impossible!

And don't you see that it is the occasional, the quality of the improbable, within an individual which sets the seal on his singularity? While you're thinking, look at me and just consider whether it isn't precisely this improbable uniqueness of an individual which an evening like this is intended to disclose.

But you get the idea! Now sit down and let me continue, for as I said, they were to meet the next evening and she was to recognize him by the flower in his lapel—a rather quaint touch, don't you think?

Such resolve! To marry that woman and no other! Yet, there was a problem. It's easy enough to make a rational decision, to choose a woman, but it's not quite so easy to resign one's heart to the choice. After all, how could he be assured of experiencing the proper passion for a woman whom he had never even seen?

This was the question he pondered as he made his way to the restaurant where they were to meet. Then, suddenly, an idea flashed through his mind: uniqueness! That was it! The specificity of passion! He had always thought of passion as an emotion directed towards the whole of an individual. But—what a notion!—perhaps passion could be made to fit the occasion. Perhaps passion could direct itself to something particular; perhaps she would have beautiful wrists, or charming lips, or exquisitely manicured fingernails or . . .

Ah! I can well imagine his elation! He would find something in this woman, something peculiar to her—and he would seize upon it. Then for once, passion would become practical, and with a bit of luck . . .

Oh, don't make the mistake of thinking me coy! I speak from my own experience. A particular passion of this sort can exist! Why, didn't I ever tell you that one evening I chose to sleep with a woman for the pure and simple reason that she was six and a half feet tall? And I tell you that my passion had force! Indeed, I have rarely experienced the emotion I knew then, lying beside her, my feet barely reaching her knees.

How different the thoughts which can drive a man! My quest, of course, stemmed from the desire to explore the diversity of nature. His motives, however, were not so pure! The years on the street had taken their toll and so he flung himself into passion in order to find peace—though what he ultimately found was a good deal more than he had bargained for!

Never had he seen such a rosy glow of well-being! Blond hair fell to her shoulders and her apple-red cheeks gave further meaning to the security which he sought. Trim and demure, she spoke quietly—but always with the strength of her convictions.

Now as to these convictions themselves . . . They were bound to the world as it was and were fostered by a middle class upbringing and comfortable surroundings. One could tell this from her clothes, her unassimilated vocabulary, and her unshaken belief in what she had been taught. My friend found that, in a way, her convictions seemed to embody something essential—something peculiar to her and yet common to the society in which she lived.

Oh, but how I search for the right expression, the proper phrase! A . . . a will . . . a will not to know! That was it! A will to ignorance!

Immediately, he was able to see that this will supported her contentment. This will made her a woman who would not put either herself or her world into question. Rather, it made her someone who was quintessentially satisfied with the continuum of the present and its truths—truths which applied to every circumstance.

Now, you mustn't misunderstand this will to ignorance! It's

not that she wouldn't occasionally see a play or read a book. That's not it at all! It was simply that she made certain that whatever she saw, whatever she read, would never threaten her world-view, or the melodious flow of her existence.

In fact, it was as if she believed that knowledge had no value save as a diversion or a practical tool. There wasn't a consumer report which she hadn't read, and she could calculate prices and profits with the speed of a computer. But in terms of a less instrumental logic, well . . . common sense is so much more reliable and, after all, doesn't ignorance lead to bliss?

Wait! We need look no further! Inadvertantly we have stumbled onto the secret logic in this methodology of ignorance. Just consider: if, from the start, intellectual curiosity is seen as disquieting at best, and positively threatening at worst, then somehow another road must be paved.

Consequently, a work of art will be enjoyed, discussed—and then shelved away. But that's not enough either, for that self-reflection which challenges the use to which practical knowledge is put must also be dismissed. You see, the will to ignorance cannot permit the least danger of conflict; there can only be *stasis.* Thus, she was a woman who never even thought of what she could be, but rather chose to love what she was.

She paved her roads with care, and put up warning signs for idealists and fools. After all, what could they offer her? The irrevocable moment? But that passes so quickly—and one might very well regret its effects for the rest of one's life. The grand experience? The odds against it are so great and besides, as my Lady herself has always maintained, one must eventually come to terms with one's inadequacies. You see, my friend, she had thought it all out, only I doubt whether she ever formulated any of it consciously.

Be that as it may, our man of the streets had met his match—to say the least! Thoroughly bewildered, he sat in front of her as these very thoughts pulsated in his mind. And then, suddenly, from the depths of his soul, an anger arose; a rage filled him which found no discernible object upon which to focus.

The anger stayed with him. Even when he awoke on the following morning, he was overcome by his fury and found himself unable to touch his breakfast. By lunchtime, the anger had not subsided and he was barely able to nibble a slice of toast or sip his *café au lait*. It was a singular anger—an anger which sought only to be perpetuated. But what could he do? He forced himself to eat some dinner in order to keep up the strength necessary to maintain his rage.

This emotional state was carried over to the following day—the day on which I met him walking the street in the late afternoon. I had never seen him in such a mood. It's true that he was never one to be overly friendly to his clients, but on the day after his meeting with this unknown woman hatred blazed in his eyes. He informed on someone with typewriters to sell and mercilessly beat up a prostitute with whom he had worked for years.

Justice, however, was not long in coming. After the last incident the entire world seemed to avoid him and by nightfall he had already had his fill.

He returned to his apartment. But after making himself dinner, he began to fidget and, within the hour, found himself walking to that woman's home. When she opened the door, she told him that she had hoped he would come. Thus, this petty hustler found himself confronted with an established relationship—a relationship which suddenly seemed as firm and sturdy as this very building in which we are sitting.

What could he have said? He was out of his element. He found himself imperceptibly drawn away from the street, and then he finally understood that there was more to his anger than the hatred of her will to ignorance.

Oh yes, he was trapped! This complacent woman with the stylish clothes had caught him. The streets were no longer his, for she had deftly managed to demand from him not only that night, but a bit more of his mortal existence as well.

Yet when he woke up in her bed on that second morning, he wasn't even groggy. No! No! In fact, he felt just wonderful lying there in that apartment with the antiseptic smell of a hospital ward.

While his eyes lazily scanned the walls, she returned from the bathroom. And what a picture she made. Although she was bouncy and fresh, with that exhausting energy of one who is trying to retrieve a long lost youth, her features still seemed anything but distinct; more exactly they appeared on the point of vanishing entirely. As a matter of fact, it seemed that she was drawing everything to her, as if she had become both the focal point and the framework of existence itself.

It was only then that he noticed the impeccable taste with which the apartment was furnished. Nothing was overdone; streamlined and comfortable, her residence radiated a clean, sharp style. She was polite and asked him if he was well. He replied that he was. They had coffee and chatted quietly in the brightly-lit kitchen.

She mentioned that she was a bit surprised that he drank as much as he had on their first evening together. For his part, he couldn't remember whether it was an exorbitant amount or not, but still he made her a promise that such a thing would never happen again.

Why did he make such a promise?

I really don't know. But I can tell you that the question plagued him for years. Even now, however, the only answer which he can come up with is that the promise made the need to explain himself superfluous. Yes, explanation was to be avoided at all costs. It was so useless, so futile! And there was always the dread that she would absorb his words and nullify the content of his thoughts.

He did not reflect upon any of this, however, as he helped her carry the dishes to the sink. Putting on her coat, she said that she would see him that evening and, as she walked out, reminded him to wash the dishes. With that, the door slammed shut and he found himself alone.

Put yourself in his place, my friend! Can't you feel the horror which she aroused by her presumptuous attitude? "See him that evening!" "Wash the dishes!" Indeed!

He resolved to have a drink as a symbol of his opposition. But unfortunately, the drink didn't help. In fact, he only felt better after watching some television. Then, deciding that he was a man of leisure with no pressing engagements, he thought it might be pleasant to lie down and relax for a while before beginning his day.

Closing his eyes, he became aware that he would fulfill his project, and yet he also felt the twinge of a desire to extricate himself from the net which was being thrown around him. Conflicting emotions wearily arose in his heart. A flush of serenity ran through him—a serenity which denied even the thought of revolt against this goal of a happy security which he had set for himself. At the same time, however, he experienced a paralyzing fear—a frightful trembling at the thought that he was being seduced.

Even a man of the street has a touch of vanity! The thought that a man such as he could be seduced was horrifying! And let me tell you, he knew that this was no ordinary seduction—with words of love, music, food and all the best that money can buy. No! No! This was a seduction of the soul based on the kindling of an inner temptation.

By then the fact was undeniable that his wife-to-be was already taking control of all that he could possibly have called his own. He realized that he had no wish to shoot pool and that even the thought of aces and kings did little to excite his imagination. He recalled that he had neatly folded the towel which he had used that morning before hanging it on the rack; it was then that he knew that the pleasures of the street were closed to him.

While washing the dishes, with an apron tied around his waist, the future came to lie bare before his eyes. His wants, his needs, his ambitions, all would be unconsciously analyzed, evaluated and fulfilled by this woman who was now his; and yet, just when he realized the full implications of his situation, he somehow felt a sense of wonder leave him.

When she arrived home for lunch, he was affable but told her nothing. With a smile, she suggested that perhaps they should go out to eat and he quickly agreed for, suddenly, the apartment seemed to become unbearably warm and stifling.

Shortly thereafter they left for the restaurant, a beautiful restaurant with antique chairs and velvet-covered walls. And I remember how he described her. Not like a goddess at all! No! She seemed to have dissolved before his eyes and turned into a gaseous substance which spread itself throughout the room, infusing itself within him, within all that space which he had once thought inviolable and his own.

Softly, gentle listener! That was how she accomplished her seduction—with a softness which hushed what remained of a voice longing to cry out! Outside there was the street with its noise and bustle . . . but it too was silenced by the woman opposite him.

Ach! That such a thing should occur! And the worst of it was that the very shrewdness of her approach, the subtlety with which she used her power, seemed to make choice impossible for her poor quarry. Yes! He believed this in his heart of hearts; that there was no choice, that he had fallen into the grips of destiny. It truly seemed that there were only illusory alternatives to this tyranny which her benevolence obscured.

My Lady understands! She can tell when sympathy is deserved! She knows that in such a situation no one can know precisely what is to be chosen, let alone the price which is to be paid. But—take it from me!—these very thoughts were not wasted on him as he left the restaurant to go home and change, so that he would look presentable while peddling his talents at the employment agencies.

Imagine his feelings of degradation! A man such as he, tossed among those small, slimy men whose mouths watered at the thought of the Judas purse which they would receive for turning another into a copy of themselves.

How I loved the description of his encounters with them—I couldn't have handled it better myself! He was honest with all of them. He mentioned his aversion to manual labor, the fact that it made him irritable and weak, that when he worked for a regular salary he couldn't sleep nights, and that he often became constipated.

But they brushed his objections aside. "Work builds character," said the first. "It's a necessary evil," said the second. "Without it, one would go mad," said the third.

Thus he returned to her apartment, job in hand. And she was thrilled! She kissed him and told him that she was proud of him, that at last he was making an effort to fulfill his real potential.

Now a hustler is never one to disregard a valid argument. So you can believe me when I tell you that he thought long and hard about the redeeming qualities of wage labor during the months in which he earned his living counting cans in a factory—a factory, by the way, which was owned by a little fat man among whose other penchants were fast cars and young men dressed in black leather.

After the first day, he came home miserably depressed. But she was able to comfort him. She would always be able to comfort him. You see, she knew that the grandest displays of emotion would never have the durability of her persistent exhibition of practical concern.

By the end of the first week, she had agreed to his proposal of marriage, although she remained virtually impassive when he broached the subject. Still, her eyebrows did curl slightly and a smile did spread across her face. In fact, she even squeezed his hand lightly with a romantic gesture. Thus, he could believe that she and he were in love. But, in the next moment, he could see it all level off into proper concern, while his own unique passion began to fade with the clear presentiment of what it would soon become.

II

Not so quick, though! The story is not yet over. No, my friend! For you see, it was only once this man of the street had achieved his goals that the real tragedy began to take shape.

While he still had his own money in his pocket he retained a semblance of independence. But the job didn't last long, and he soon found himself living off her income—living at her mercy. She bought his clothes and told him what to wear, gave him pocket money and told him how to spend it, asked him questions and expected answers.

The noose grew tighter as day followed day in the monotonous routine of her tyranny—which was worse than anything he might have expected. Indeed, even that sense of repulsive fascination for her complacent competence vanished and, little by little, his cynical sense of superiority gave way to the attitude of a servile clerk. In short, he grew not only to loathe her, but to fear her as well. Gradually they found less and less to say to one another. Finally, they were reduced to silence, there, in her apartment, where they sat night after night while her belly slowly began to expand.

No! He couldn't take his eyes off her, and sometimes he even thought that his luck would change. He thought that with the birth of a child he might yet be rescued from his existence of silence, security, boredom, comfort—and rain.

For during those days it rained constantly. Time passed and still it rained—against the walls, against the windows, with a steady patter that almost drowned the shrill cries outside which virtually echoed his own discontentment.

Everywhere there were shouts of anger, screams of outrage. But he remained alone with her; he left his apartment only rarely. Yet he could sense it all outside and he felt the revolt tempting him. Still, he resisted the impulse to join the mob whose shouting never ceased.

He and his wife always sat by the window looking out, barely able to see because of the rain, and he would listen to her exclamations of horror. She was appalled. Anarchy! Chaos in the streets! The fall of law and order and the rise of barbarism! It was as if she were experiencing an insult to her very existence.

But he grew ever more curious. Sometimes he wanted to go out, if only to assert himself against his wife. Nevertheless, every time he put on his coat, he realized that he owed it to her; he realized that his comfortable sofa was hers, that the food on his table was hers. Everything was hers—and he lived so well! After thinking these thoughts, he would curse himself and mumble that he was too old for rebellion, take up his seat by the window, and go back to listening to the shouting and the rain.

I've never seen it rain like that again! Torrents and torrents of rain battered the shabby coats and jackets which the mob wore in that city so far away. But still, they yelled their slogans as the rain and the billyclubs fell. He heard them day after day; sometimes the cries seemed to come from farther away, sometimes it sounded as if a holocaust were taking place in front of his building.

But what did it mean to the two of them? They had their own worries! They had a nursery to pay for, a child on the way, and those unique problems which each posed for the other. They had no time for mobs or the havoc that fools set loose.

And yet they could not shut out the dulling, deadening screams. The screaming became part of their lives, and he saw his wife's face stiffen amid the shouting, the retching, the blood, the cramps and the drugs she was given. She became ever more irritable and the power which she held became ever more manifest. He had given up the streets, but still she criticized his language, his drinking and, of course, his laziness.

He bore it all silently. But he began to think of that lump in her belly, of the existence it would lead in the family which this child could not choose. When she became ill late in her pregnancy and the doctor reported that the child might be born as a vegetable, his emotions were mixed—though the first word he uttered was "abortion."

But this woman, with her common sense and conventional wisdom, refused to take life so lightly. She called religion to her aid, morality to her side—and it all meant nothing to him. Thus, for various reasons, they took opposing viewpoints and . . .

Quite right, my Love! It's true enough! She had never seen the streets and he had never left them. And, on the streets, one plays the odds and expects the worst; there is never room for optimism. For her, on the other hand, there was never a place for anything that might shake the foundations of her contentment. So, where she could picture only a gurgling infant at her breast, he could only see the image of an idiot—and an expensive idiot at that!

You find him callous, dearest listener?

Well, if I may say so, perhaps that's because you can afford your sensitive humanism. Oh! I see you, my friend! I've picked you for a reason! I look at you, and its easy to see that you've put on a little weight over the last year or two—and you can always get the sense of a man's worth by the size of his paunch.

Just look at you! How comfortable you are! Sitting there, in your chair, a drink by your side, lifting the cigarette to your lips, with a quizzical look in your eyes, careful not to let the ash fall on your tailored pants.

As for me, I would have been very much surprised had he not thought of the extra money which such a child would cost. Don't you know by now that there is always a hidden factor in the choices which a person makes?

Humanity! Human nature! Nonsense! Tell me the thoughts of a man before he acts, then tell me the actions which he performs, and I'll tell you the type of world which has taught him what he knows. Just give me the rich man, the poor man, the poor man made rich and the rich man made poor, put each face to face with love or death and you'll see soon enough how they differ!

They argued for weeks and weeks. He tried to explain himself again and again, make her understand that he wanted only the best for all concerned, and yet she could give only one response. Whether from high-mindedness or stupidity, she resolved that: "I will not be the instrument of death."

And what is one to say to that, eh? All that he could do was turn his back and feel the skin on her face growing taut, her eyes glistening, her lips pursing to form the word: murderer.

She had wanted to speak the word from the very beginning, from the moment he had raised the subject of abortion, but she had held herself back. Yet, of course, the word was finally spoken and when he heard it there was no alternative left for him but to return to the streets of that historic city, hunt for his contacts, and start all over again.

But—except for myself—no one was to be found. He sought them out everywhere, but they were silent when he accosted them in cafés, refused when he wished to buy them drinks in bars, and furious when he disturbed them in whorehouses. There was nothing to be done; when he met them they brushed him aside, when he called them he heard only the click of the phone in his ear.

You see, dearest listener, such a man makes few friends. He is generally viewed as a parasite and his best customer is always the one who is suffering the most. These customers never forget. In the past when he had organized the drugs and the women for an evening, he had made his clients bleed. Thus, when they were given the chance, they made him bleed in turn.

He stood in empty alleyways for weeks, but no one came. Then someone informed the police of his reappearance and of his connection with some theft of which he was entirely ignorant. Thus, he had to remain on his guard and emerge only in the early hours of the morning.

Gradually he came to realize that he could not continue, that he would have to leave. But first he came to see me, for my door is never closed to anyone and my words are there for all to hear.

That evening he brought a bottle which we shared like brothers. He spoke to me of the child, that child whom he believed to be deformed, still deep in the cavern of the woman he despised. He spoke of justice and faith, of hope and luck, of happiness and security, and the words made little sense. I could see that he was on the verge of a mental collapse and so I suggested that he might visit her at the hospital, for the child was about due.

At first he was enraged, he wouldn't hear of it. But, during the days which followed, the thought of that child never left him. Finally, he said that he would never forgive himself if he didn't find out what had happened to that woman who once was his and that child whom he would never know.

During those days we spent together, during those hours in which we walked, we barely noticed the rain that came hurtling at us, so absorbed were we in our thoughts. The broken windows, the red tinge to the water which flowed along the curb to the sewer meant nothing. There were only what he perceived as his own peculiar, singular concerns. All of them seemed scrambled together: there was the persistent need for happiness, the price he had paid for an illusory security, his unemployment, the thought of his child, the recollection of the doctor's brusque manner, and the way he spoke of that being as if it were a thing.

What could those people on the streets know of all this? After all, it had nothing to do with them; whatever their demands, they had nothing to do with him. Besides, even if they did know, the one lesson he had learned on the streets was that no one could be trusted.

When we left the hospital on a cold rainy morning he was still talking about the problems which plagued him. The demonstrators were still everywhere and, with every block that we walked, people called out for us to join them. But we passed on, hands in our pockets, collars pulled up against the rain.

Still, we couldn't help seeing what was happening in those streets which both of us knew so well. A myriad of policemen, some on horseback and some on foot, spread out to encircle the mob. At given points, however, some of the rebels would break through the net and the police would have to pull back, retrench, and attempt to implement their strategy all over again.

They started over countless times and, wherever we walked, it was easy to see that the same tactics were being employed. Finally, however, the police drew up and launched the first wedge straight into the heart of the mass. The demonstrators dispersed, ran in every direction, and gathered together in small groups. The police advanced again—and then it began in earnest. A woman was dragged across the street by her hair and one could see blood streaming over the hands of a man who was holding his temples. Clothes were torn, bodies fell to the ground, circulars were scattered on the wet sidewalk—but the slogans continued to ring in our ears.

Yet, there were still my friend's unique concerns . . . and the child. Besides, what could we have done to combat the blue uniforms and glistening helmets in their attack upon those of whom we were not a part?

Suddenly, however, a woman shrieked as she was kicked and her eyes fell upon us. She was kicked again and again, and in her face there was the half-crazed look of a tortured animal. She reached out to us and begged for help as the rains fell.

But we didn't move. We stood as we were. Transfixed and helpless, I saw my Lady smirking from an open manhole and, for a moment, I thought that I had caught sight of the little monster looking out from the other side of a closed window.

Oh! How right you are, my Love!

For one who has actually experienced the monster at its height, all the screams must have seemed petty indeed; the dabs of blood spilled in the rain formed but a drop of the ocean which the monster had once sucked from the throats of its victims.

Of course! The mob never really knew the monster. But still, those youths and workers did show us a modicum of—certainly misplaced—courage. For none of those people had ever known real violence. The very thought of spilt blood should have been menacing enough—and yet it wasn't!

How naive they were! Men in uniform charged and the protestors fled until they were forced to fight. They had no battle plan and they never even attempted to take over strategic targets. No! They were interested in *symbolic action*. And what an army they made! An army without generals or guns, wading through the water, bending down to pick up their wounded instead of pushing on . . . But they always returned! From the crevices of the street, from the alleys, from beneath parked cars, from empty hallways, they would emerge like rats and reassemble, only to be thrown back again.

We watched it all as the rain soaked us to the skin. A brick seemed to appear miraculously before our feet and my companion picked it up. A policeman was standing over a long-haired, dirty young man, his boot digging into the youth's back, his billyclub raised to . . .

But what did I see?! I looked to my side and I saw my

friend, brick in hand, drawing back his arm and aiming at the policeman's head.

Thank God, my Darling, that you appeared when you did! I caught your glance and I did as you would have asked. I grabbed his wrist, a second before he would have let the brick fly—and heard the young man's screams pierce my ears.

My companion turned to me angrily and told me that I had no right to interfere. After a moment or two, however, his face covered with shame, he added that I was probably right, that the very idea of conflict was ridiculous, that a powerful state structure could not be fought, and that it would all soon be forgotten anyway like some gangfight in a ghetto.

Nevertheless, it was with a certain sadness that he finally let the brick fall to the ground; clearly he was not as satisfied with the decision as he should have been. I'm sure he was thinking of his child, his idiot child, and he was uneasy as we entered the underground station and walked to the platform. There we looked into the black tunnel, waiting for it to fill up with the lights of a speeding train. The smell of urine reached our nostrils while around us drunkards were lying on the benches and insects were crawling along the walls.

The noise was excruciating as the train arrived. Yes! The sound was such that, when I looked at my companion, I saw that finally—for just an instant—he was freed from the screaming in the streets which had plagued him for so very long.

When we entered the hospital, however, that momentary freedom was lost. Once we had made our way through the exit, which led directly to the hospital basement, there was not a soul to be seen and not a sound to be heard. It seemed to take an endless amount of time to find a nurse who would give us directions to his wife's room. Then, cautiously, we followed the winding corridors until we came to the ward, a gray hole equally divided by six beds.

Dearest friend! Listen closely: one girl is groaning spasmodically, grasping the edges of her blanket with the little strength which her fingers still possess. Look carefully: the one next to her doesn't move; the only way one can tell that she's alive is by the plastic tube which has been pushed up her nose and which is registering her body fluids with a monotonous click. There you can see an old woman reading, who, with every other sentence, is shifting her eyes to the window. Beside her lie two more women who gossip quietly while their crushed limbs hang suspended in plaster casts.

And she . . . she was lying alone, partially drugged and passive, facing the wall. Immediately, he walked over to her bed and stared at her back. She turned towards him and, with half-shut eyes amid the stink of death, finally spoke. There was only a sentence, or maybe two, which I could make out: the child is normal, you are no longer necessary.

From the other end of the ward I could feel him shudder. Yet his lips didn't move. She watched him for a moment or two and then turned away. He began to move towards me after what seemed like an endless moment, and we walked out together.

There was no idiot, there was only a slave—a slave whom he would never see: an innocent who would enter her grasp, who would be formed and taught by her, who would be infused by her being. Yes! Thoughts of the idiot vanished and were replaced by thoughts of the slave—the child born into chains.

We walked back through the same corridors, only we looked more closely. The paint was peeling off the walls and we saw a body covered by a white sheet lying on a stretcher in a doorway. We noticed people waiting in line in front of a desk: one shivering, the next unable to keep himself from coughing, another sitting on a chair, an infected blister exposed on her foot. We saw them waiting patiently as a youth was wheeled past, his face black and blue, and we heard the sounds of a policeman cursing in the background.

Finally, once again, we found ourselves on the subway platform. But this time there was no exhilaration as the train approached. Thoughts of the slave, of a new being entering our world, filled our minds as we observed a bum sleeping with his legs stretched out across a seat which had been slashed. A few seats further down, a bored and tired man in a business suit was sitting upright with his tie hanging loosely from an unbuttoned collar, while a woman of quality was dabbing her neck with a cheap perfume whose fragrance filled the air. It became unbearably hot and we hardly noticed the soot, the newspapers strewn around the floor, and the empty bottle of cheap wine which rolled back and forth with the swaying motion of the train.

I glanced over at my companion and I could see his face filled with grief. But no! There was more than grief! There was horror as well! I couldn't help feeling that somehow he was experiencing the world for the very first time—that he was becoming conscious of an aesthetic revulsion. Yes, I could see a hatred taking shape in his eyes for that world of ugliness, illness, complacency and misery in which his own existence had been formed and which his child, that slave, would inherit.

And I knew that he desperately wanted to find them again, those who made up that mob with its half-formulated demands for a new world! Oh! I'm sure that he thought of the brick! Even I was forced to picture that girl being pulled by her hair imploring us to help her, and that young man with the blood streaming from his temples running down over his hands, and that policeman bending over the demonstrator with his club raised high.

But it was too late. Of course, neither of us knew it at the time. You see, in the subway, I suddenly felt my companion's face begin to glow. Yet, as we went through the exit, we heard no screams and the streets were devoid of hope. For the sun had finally emerged from the clouds and the rain had stopped. The weather was beautiful and one could even see the first couples venturing out into the evening for a stroll.

The two of us watched them for a few moments. Then we separated. But I couldn't help thinking of the despair that was surely in his heart. A warm night was coming on and those whom he sought had disappeared. How very sad that his anger, his will to freedom, had come too late, that he had missed his chance to participate in actualizing a dream.

And it became clear to me that there was nothing left for him in that city so very far from our own and that he would have to leave. But where was he to go? The revolt had passed and everything seemed so very dismal. I knew that he would convince himself that there was nothing more to do. It was then I understood that everything which had taken place would only emerge as another story in a new city with new streets and a new café.

Epilogue

The world turns into dream, the dream into world
And what you believe you've left behind you
Still approaches from afar to find you.

—Novalis

SO we return to our café! Now you know what my reflections were on that night and you too have seen fantasies glimmering in the dusk. Yet even after the stories had been told, after the recollections had passed, I remained seated for a little while longer. I sat quietly, absorbed in my thoughts. But one can never sit still for too long—after all, nature's call is a strong distraction. As I entered the bathroom, I saw my little fat friend leaning against the open door to one of the toilets, fingering that lovely tiepin which once was mine. Hurriedly, I relieved myself. But still, I couldn't help noticing how the lamplight was falling through the small square window on the ceiling. Indeed, it threw a supernatural glow over his head, as it outlined his shadow, which seemed to stain the floor.

What a sight he was! Beads of sweat were suspended on his brow and he stammered when he finally spoke. Thus it was only hesitantly, with a throttled cry in his throat, that he asked me if I would care to join him for about a quarter of an hour—behind closed doors.

Oh! I didn't take offense! I was even touched in a way that he should have made the offer. But though I did stare at the tiepin for a moment or two, I refused. After all, I knew that I had an appointment with my Lady and I would never want to disappoint her. Still, I made haste to add that he should ignore me and feel free to act as his passions demanded.

I began to wash my hands, as I listened to him letting down his trousers. On hearing the latchdoor shut, however, I happened to glance into the mirror above the sink. I was transfixed by what I saw and the moans from behind me receded from my world.

As I think now of what I saw then! . . The truth chokes my words! It was . . . It was a man growing old.

Grey hair, streaked with silver, was plastered to his skull, barely touching the white silk scarf tied around his neck. Purple bags hung from his eyes and crow's feet were spreading at the socket's edges. Holding his cane, he raised his hand to his face, and his eyes grew wide as he noticed how fat his fingers had become and how feverishly they clung to the black metal handle of the walking stick. His gaze was filled with intensity and, whether it was from embarrassment or fear, the right side of his face began to twitch. Under a long brown coat with a velvet collar, he wore what was left of a three piece suit. The cuffs which protruded were frayed and the rhinestone cufflinks were garish. The jacket was gone and the vest was spotted.

A battered dandy stared at me and I knew that it was I! Yet this image was as alien to me as . . . as that broad black hat which lay in tatters on his head like a discarded laurel.

Oh! How I searched for even the hint of a resemblance with what I imagined myself to be! But I found none. And still it was me! Yet could this actually have been me? Me! The choice of my choices, in all my manhood?

As what did I appear? A shabby bohemian, a parasite, and nothing more. Thank God for my Lady! She taught me what I know and I know now that I am more than what I appear to be, more than what my choices have made me! . . After all, a man is always more than he appears to be, more than what he does!

But it took me a while to assimilate her knowledge. At the time, I wished only to know what had become of those choices I had made—they seemed so very few.

For I tell you that once I had wanted more! Where were those choices from which I could not choose? Where were those options that were never presented? Why? Why had they been denied me?

It was then that the thought of the irrevocable act, the grand experience, came to mind. I wondered: was the world so very perfect, so very full, that this act should no longer be considered necessary? I turned back to the mirror: a poet of the gutter, a man of the street.

No! The action needs to be taken even now! It should already have been taken! The old man had chosen and the little guard had forfeited his choice; my little actress had activated the dream while the dreamer had only dreamed; the listener had acted and was torn by remorse while a man of the streets was regretting and beginning to forget what had slipped through his fingers. Oh! That hustler! At least he had the chance . . . Yet, even if one has the chance, where does one find the will to act?

Ach! Don't bother me with the child! Where did it get him?

But no! Wait! Don't misunderstand! I too wished to fight! I too wanted justice and equality and happiness! But there were never any Spains for me and Chile went too fast! . . Oh! What had become of that action of which others had so boldly dreamed? What had become of it? I reflected on the image before me: a beggar, a bohemian relegated to wine and words.

Ah! I'm sorry! But it's not to be helped. The force of habit overcomes me! I think of yet another story which I was told in this very place.

Tell me, my friend, did you know that among certain primitive tribes a legend exists regarding a certain sacred stone? They say that the stone is transparent, clearer than the freshest spring. They say that it's small and yet that it always exactly fills the palm of whomever holds it. To this day it has never been found. But, the savages claim that, were it to be held for even a second, it would allow the possessor to relive a moment of his past.

Just think! A man could choose freely! For once there would be no restrictions! Everything would be disclosed! All the moments which memory had buried would surface and then . . .

How patient you seem, my Darling! You wait so quietly for me to continue. But on that night, if I remember correctly, you were not quite so patient!

No! No! Your face appeared behind me right in the midst

of my thoughts. You interrupted my thoughts and your face glared hideously in the mirror like the face of some graffiti-covered madonna.

How well I remember your lips touching my ear! How well I recall the feeling of worms crawling along my skin, and my eyes closing, and my head drooping backwards until finally all those thoughts which had begun to take shape in my mind became distorted and grotesque.

I tremble when I think of it! You, a lady of misery and I, a man of sense; the two of us, flung together by an unopposed destiny—a special, unalterable destiny which denies the act along with the perception of its need.

Fool that I was! I thought then that it was the world which had done this to me. Now, of course, I know better . . . But I tell you that I never hated you as I hated you then! And you knew it—and you made me pay! Do you remember how my body writhed under your grimy fingers, how my yellow teeth chattered and how you tried to suck the hopes from my mind.

You forced me to look at the cubicle; the drone of the little fat one's sighs were growing louder. Above the crumpled garments around his feet, I saw his legs: spindly, dirty and misshapen. I turned to you and you sat there grinning. Then I understood: whereas you touch men such as myself with your lips, there are a vast host of others whom you beat with your staff.

"Why them and not me?" I thought to myself, and a shiver ran down my body. There was no reason at all!

Arbitrary bitch that you are: You let me know that I wouldn't be safe—ever! That, just like the force of history, at any moment you could turn me into one of them.

Like the listener! Can you imagine, my friend?

I never was so shaken as at that moment! And yet, from that overpowering fear, a new dream seemed to jut out from my thoughts like a broken tooth on a child's face. Yes, I felt that thrill of comprehension which my little actress had once so fully experienced! A vibrant hope arose and, for a moment, it seemed to foreshadow the time when I would revolt against this elusive tyrant's whims.

How I hated her, dearest companion! How I wanted to scream out! But I checked myself; I was alone.

If only you had been there! Then we could have begun to prepare, prepare to conquer her together! Yes! You and I, and then a hundred million others in a great assault upon her and her hidden legion of sycophants. Then, my friend, the grand experience would finally have become ours! We would have conquered history and subdued the horror of an arbitrary destiny! A world of our own would have opened before our eyes and, at last, we might have become what we have always dreamt that we were.

Oh, were I only able, were you only there! We could have wrung her leather-like neck! And then, as her eyes would have begun to roll into her skull, the first creation could have commenced. The moment without end! The time without masters or slaves! It would have marked the end of ugliness and the beginning of a period of active freedom and dignity for each of us! All this could have begun at that moment!

What an irrevocable act that would have been, eh? In art and philosophy dreams have been laid out for us, they have been structured and described for an open future. And at that moment, we just might have begun to actualize all that which we have been taught in distorted forms!

Imagine! From all those unfulfilled wishes and hopes of the past, not one would have been forgotten! And think of it! Finally something new would have been brought into the world. A new right! A positive right! A right, potentially more powerful than any other; a right to create for ourselves, a right to beauty!

It's not so crazy! What did those mobs chant? *"Power to the Imagination!" "Demand the Impossible!"* I remembered thinking of that character in the old man's story, the poor fellow with the gushing dream. I thought of him and of the old man's sparkle and, for once, I too wished to see the sun soaked in wine and the clouds bathed in gold.

Beauty stripped naked, standing on the streets! Fantasy made bare and manifest in our lives! This was the world which I wished to see, a world in which the reciprocal power of the imagination would color all the space which separates each of us from the others.

It's true, my friend! The world awoke when I thought of the beauty which could be and of the action by which we would realize what tradition has taught us to be nothing other than a matter of privilege or taste. Oh! To smash that will to ignorance!

But I was alone and so hopes for the new world gave way to thoughts of an inexorable, arbitrary destiny. Alone, I was denied the collective historical action which I craved and so the world as it was became immutable once again, while the future weighed on my breast like a leaden passion.

Then, my ragged love, I looked at you with new eyes! The outside world became closed to me and you drew me inwards! There, inside myself, I looked at my existence in a new light, a brighter light!

As I stood bewildered and confused, a man without alternatives, you opened your arms and embraced me. Then you led me to the sanctuary where I still remain, the sanctuary which I have been able to create in the quietude of an inner reprieve.

Just look around you, my friend! Behold what I have created! My café! My little world in which I can make my home and live out my life by weaving together strands from the lives of those whom I encounter.

Indeed! While the monster lurked outside, I discovered my destiny. Not much of a destiny—that I grant you!—but at least one in which I feel safe and secure.

Precisely at that moment, however, I heard the deep sigh of orgasm coming from the toilet—a languishing sound which still lingers in my ear. But I remember more! I remember how my Lady stopped running her hands up and down my legs and how my head fell forward and how my eyes became fixed on the floor where I noticed the clumps of a half-white liquid slowly coagulating.

A last moment of disgust, of rebellion, overcame me. And so, I rushed from that bathroom which stank with the intangible remains of a thousand patrons. I found myself in the café once again, my mouth dry and my movements stiff. A fever, which my friend the listener must have experienced upon looking at that innocent child, descended upon me. A blissful oblivion of anger took hold of me and, with all my strength, I raised my cane above my head and . . .

Dazed, I remember lifting myself up from the sidewalk and returning inside. Quietly, I made my apologies as I sensed my Lady nodding her head in approval. Wearily, I sat down at my table; a waitress, the same waitress who works here now, came over to serve me.

I looked at her and thought of the hustler's wife. I could see that for this woman the present was a plenitude in which the tension between *what is* and *what can be* was subsumed in the healthy contentment of an eternal *stasis.*

Instantly, desire welled up in my heart. Yes, it's true and, what's more, my Lady couldn't have been happier. Once again, without a sound, my Lady turned up behind me and I felt the palm of her hand affectionately squeezing my shoulder.

How proud I was of that passion which I thought was dead! But, though I basked in its pleasure, I couldn't help feeling that the moment without end was giving way to its epigone. That moment, the moment which I wanted to create with you and a hundred million others like you, was deflated into an instant which existed for myself alone. Indeed, it turned into one moment amongst others—nothing special at all.

But, perhaps it could still be made special! Perhaps I might . . . It was then that the inspiration overcame me! A tale! A story which I would narrate and which my listener would interpret!

How's that for building a community? How's that for overcoming the solitude of experience which that little country girl, from ages ago, could never express!?!

Yes, I decided that if I could not act, then I would at least make the best of my inaction. I would create a living fiction for myself through narrating the needs and dreams of others. And what a fiction it would be! A fiction which would protect me from the poverty of this world without action! A fiction which would draw strangers to me and let them bask in my destiny!

Oh, I tell you that my heart was aglow with an anticipation which became ever stronger. For through those stories, and in the rapture of my listeners, I would finally show myself to be more than what circumstances had made of me. Perhaps, for a time, the world might even become what I had always wished it to be. But then I glanced at you, my loathsome Love, and my soul contracted with an ecstatic anguish as I suddenly understood just how close we were as well as how much closer we would become.

Of course, the waitress knew nothing of this! She spoke to me in a voice full of curiosity and cynical concern, and it was only with great difficulty that I managed to control my heavy breathing.

The step had to be taken then if it was ever to be taken at all! Thus, hurriedly, practically forcing the words out of my mouth, I began to tell my very first tale, the story of my two cats.

What a primitive tale it was! And yet, how I loved those furry little animals! You see, they were homosexual and very much in love. In fact, theirs was a love which completely enveloped their lives. As fate would have it, however, one of them died of pneumonia—and the other's choice was made. At first he sulked, hid in a corner, and contemplated his loneliness. He grew thin and listless and spent most of his time brooding. After a week, he threw himself under the wheels of an onrushing automobile; thus, my sensitive, unique, little creature turned into an everyday suicide.

As I was finishing my story, I saw the beginnings of a smile on the waitress's lips. I could see that she wished to hear more, but she rose from her seat and said that she had to get back to work. She began to walk back to the bar, but then, suddenly, she turned and threw me a sly wink.

It was only to be expected that my Lady should have vanished for the moment. What else could I do but think about this woman, this waitress, who had listened to my very first story? What callousness! That she could leave me with hardly a word when my new existence was hanging in the balance!

But, upon further reflection, I realized that such actions are not out of the ordinary. Why, the very night before, I had heard this very same woman describing to a crude bartender how she had wept—can you imagine?—upon hearing a song which evoked some memories from the past.

Yes, I remember that she spoke with an emotion which was heartrending. Yet, across from her at the bar, a man was sitting, gazing at her with the most pitiful expression of longing.

Naturally, she didn't even notice him—but I did. The man reminded me of the little prison guard. How timid he seemed! Far too hesitant to make an advance! Oh! I could see how silence would save him from the embarrassment of rejection, the anguish of failure, the need for choice.

Poor man that he was! I could see desire burning in his eyes. But he drank calmly, with the steadiness of one who is in no hurry to act upon a decision which has somehow already been made. Yes, he drank silently in order to overcome the fear which constrained him. Indeed, he drank with the patience of one who is building a ship in a bottle, an island of resistance against the cruelty of an imaginary sea. I looked at him and I knew that he was a man of illusions—that he too would succumb to the vision of my Lady's garden where only the ghosts dance.

He took the ghosts with him when he left, for within two hours the fellow had slipped out of the bar unobserved. He had not spoken to her and he was never seen again. But I know that one day he will regret his cowardice. Then, like the hustler, he will think of what might have been; then his island of silence will stick in his throat and he will try to scream.

Of course, you are right, dearest listener!

By then it will be too late! But what a scream that will be! Can you imagine him, this little fellow, standing there like a vision incarnate of that maniac Munch!?! For he too will have to hold his hands to his ears and I can see his eyes flaming like redhot coals while the waves of sound turn into colors that wrap themselves around him! But with that scream . . .

Oh! *The new* is always introduced with a scream, with the anguish of a joy which is yet to come. Only through the scream will the world as it is start to crack; only through the scream will this little man feel that he is taking part in the act which will mark the destruction of the garden in which ghosts continue to dance.

Yes! I see now that even the scream has its promise which brands the search for that which is unnameable . . .But wait! It is not unnameable! The name is given and it is given by me! Yes, by me! In each tale, in every story, in each tone and in every pause, through what is said and by what remains to be said, the outlines always appear of *that which is not!*

And it's true! With the idea of *what is not* the present begins to totter! The future awaits, bold and vibrant—and look my friend! My Lady is finally trembling! She's scared to death! She knows that I have found her weakness!

Just look at you, my Love! Rattle the chains of the present and panic runs through your veins! Now think of the stories, my Angel! For through them, perhaps a bit of that glistening fabric of tomorrow will be woven.

So now you're listening, eh? Well, listen close!

Change! Do you hear the word, my Darling!?!

Tremble, my Angel! Tremble!

Think! Perhaps through these stories the idea may arise that change is possible! That it's necessary! That a new world calls to us from the truth in those stories of the past!

Why, my friend, even now I think that a story told to a stranger at least allows one to believe that an imprint on the world has been made! That such an imprint can be made! That it must be made by each of us—each of us who changes the story with every telling and who thereby expands the truth of what is yet to come.

Be damned, my Love!

All right! So perhaps not everyone changes a story in terms of what is to come! So what if a few individuals use a story for themselves alone? Why shouldn't the first suppose himself a little braver, the second a little more generous, the third a little more daring, and the fourth a little wiser than he really is? So what if a few people live with illusions? After all, a few suppositions must be made!

My God! One must have a bit of feeling for human frailty! You can't expect too much! After all, we can't actualize as yet the dream of what is to come! No, not as yet! People have to eat! People have to work! People need a little comfort from the entertainment which a story can give! It's foolish to be hasty! We must wait for the proper time, we must be prudent, for...

And what is that sigh you breathe so deeply, my Lady!

I have... we have... our stories... and...

That poodle is nuzzling at my leg once again! There's a sound in my ear and I hear you whispering, my Love... Oh! How wonderful it is to feel your embrace! How wonderful to be back in your arms!

There, my Love! I'm yours once more! You know that I never really meant those horrible things I said! It was all in the manner of a . . . of a . . . story! Yes! A story! A tale! Only a tale! For I would never desert you! There's too much time, much too much time...

Why, you're blushing, my Love! How romantic I feel! Not at all like that night when I stepped out of the café into the early morning.

How very sad it was, with the moon hanging like a lantern in a violet sky which still held a few remaining stars. I remember concluding that it must have rained only a little while earlier for the pavement was damp and my feet were unbearably cold. I watched the stars in a melancholy trance as I walked along the river's edge, beyond which I could see the lights still sparkling on the opposite shore. But dawn was breaking, and yet when the moon glimmered I thought for the last time that I might just be able to act in order that...

What a horrible moment of ambivalence! But then I felt a woman's touch. Leaning against me, her lips came close to my neck as she quietly said that now, if I had the time to talk, she had the time to listen. I saw the waitress standing before me and I breathed deeply so that my lungs could fill themselves with the crisp night air.

Oh please, my Love! Will you stop pulling at my sleeve!

Ah, I see! Yes! Yes! I do see her at the bar adding up the check!

Ahem! Well, you must excuse me, my friend. I'm in no rush but, as you can see, my Lady wishes to depart. No need to get up!

Aha! She's spotted me!

Oh! But I simply must dash! . . We really must get together again in the future! But for now, I can only tip my hat, thank you for a marvelous evening, and bid you a very fond *adieu!*